PENGUIN MODERN CLASSICS

A Drop of Blood

JOGINDER PAUL (1925–2016) was a highly renowned and award-winning writer of Urdu fiction. A writer of both short stories and novels, Paul was an important figure in the Progressive Writers' Movement, and his work has garnered praise and popularity in the realm of Urdu literature. *Ek Boond Lahoo Ki* (published in Penguin Classics as *A Drop of Blood*) was his first novel and remains one of his most significant works.

SNEHAL SHINGAVI is associate professor of English at the University of Texas, Austin, and the author of *The Mahatma Misunderstood: The Politics and Forms of Literary Nationalism in India* (2013). He has also translated Munshi Premchand's Hindi novel *Sevasadan* (2005), the Urdu short-story collection *Angaaray* (Penguin, 2014), Bhisham Sahni's autobiography, *Today's Pasts* (Penguin, 2015) and Agyeya's *Shekhar: A Life* (Penguin, 2017; co-translated with Vasudha Dalmia). He has also been published widely in publications like *GQ India*, the *International Socialist Review*, *Postcolonial Text*, *South Asia* and the *Annual of Urdu Studies*.

JOGINDER PAUL

A Drop of Blood

Translated by Snehal Shingavi

PENGUIN BOOKS

An imprint of Penguin Random House

PENGUIN BOOKS

USA | Canada | UK | Ireland | Australia
New Zealand | India | South Africa | China | Singapore

Penguin Books is part of the Penguin Random House group of companies
whose addresses can be found at global.penguinrandomhouse.com

Published by Penguin Random House India Pvt. Ltd
4th Floor, Capital Tower 1, MG Road,
Gurugram 122 002, Haryana, India

First published in Penguin Books by Penguin Random House India 2020

10 9 8 7 6 5 4 3 2

ISBN 9780143450160

Typeset in Adobe Caslon Pro by Manipal Technologies Limited, Manipal

Printed at Repro India Limited

www.penguin.co.in

This is a legitimate digitally printed version of the book and therefore might not
have certain extra finishing on the cover.

CONTENTS

PREFACE

BLOOD THAT IS RARE ...

Ek Boond Lahoo Ki by Joginder Paul was written in Nairobi in the late fifties when Nehruvian socialism was very much in the air in India and the author was greatly affected by class inequalities witnessed in Kenya. I have often wondered what may have triggered the author to choose the theme of buying and selling of blood. Was there any personal story of poverty, unemployment and desperation behind it? The author after all was himself a penniless refugee when he migrated to Kenya after the Partition of 1947. I believe my recent probe into my ninety-year-old mother's memory bank has given me the answer. The seed of the novel was sown in all likelihood when my mother, who incidentally possesses the same rare blood type as that of the protagonist of the novel, suffered a near-death experience due to the paucity of blood at a Kenyan hospital where she had to undergo a surgical procedure in 1957. The doctor had declared no hope for her survival and the mourning had all but started when a young man suddenly appeared to offer his own matching blood and my mother was saved. The trauma stayed with the family and in my father's writerly mind worked itself out creatively in the form of the novel *Ek Boond Lahoo Ki* in Urdu. As it were, a deeply personal feeling acquired a completely impersonal attire. The novel was first published in 1962 in Karachi. There is no trace or reference whatsoever to the personal context in the narrative, but I know that my father was emotionally attached to this novel like to no other book of his.

About a year and a half ago, when Snehal Shingavi from Texas communicated his wish to translate this novel, I was taken aback. How did he get a copy of this novel? Well, thankfully much of our literatures seem to lie preserved in some American university library or the other. The novel in Urdu is not available in India. The translation of the novel is a result of Snehal's own initiative and therefore bears the mark of both love as well as rigour. *A Drop of Blood*—the English avatar of the Urdu *Ek Boond Lahoo Ki*—would have greatly pleased the author. Often had he wished for a wider dissemination of the vision of this novel: the publication of *A Drop of Blood* will hopefully do that. Even today, many get caught between poverty and conscience, and they trade in blood and human organs; and many die as unacknowledged poor martyrs, if only to save the lives of the rich. The novel remains relevant and is reborn in Snehal Shingavi's English translation to relate to today's world.

Sukrita Paul Kumar

TRANSLATOR'S NOTE

Joginder Paul's first novel, *A Drop of Blood* (*Ek Boond Lahoo Ki*), was a remarkable debut for a writer whose career went on to span several decades. It provides several clues as to what animated his writing and how it would develop. Early signals of his later works are evident here—an interest in the multi-confessional character of India; the use of myth and epic structure; the strangeness of having corpses, roads and cars speak as if they were characters. From any post-Independence perspective, however, the fact that Paul, a Hindu, chose Urdu as the medium of his expression exposes two fallacies at the same time: first, that language has a religion (a commonly held misconception in South Asia today); and second, that Urdu could not successfully modernize itself. This is part of the reason that Paul's writing is so important and has endured for so long and with so much success.

But *Ek Boond Lahoo Ki* poses very interesting problems that are unique to the novel and perhaps to the moment in which it was written. It was published in 1962 at the dying end of the Nehruvian era but expressed some of its most deeply held pieties: a socialist dispensation for India, tolerance of all religious expression, a hope for the uplift of women, and modernized and educated life for all of its citizens. In order to capture that, Paul's novel deals with, among others, a secular Rajput protagonist, a Hindu/Sikh elderly woman with little education, an Anglo-Indian nurse, an ultra-modern Muslim doctor and his daughter, a married Muslim woman and her husband, a Hindu clerk, and a range of other minor characters. What is so daunting about the novel is that, perhaps other than Qurratulain Hyder's *Aag Ka Darya* (*River of Fire*), no other novel has made a self-conscious attempt to include so many different kinds of voices from so many different communities. Even Premchand was able, at best, to do two or three at a time.

This, however, is the greatest challenge for a translator. The main character, Mohan, speaks a very plain sort of Urdu, only occasionally punctuated with English, since that was his main subject of study in college. His adopted mother, Bebe, speaks in a rustic idiom, which is neither Punjabi nor Rajasthani (Paul was from Sialkot) but an idiosyncratically non-standard Urdu designed to give the feel of a recently urbanized villager. Bele Rina, the Anglo-Indian nurse, speaks with an Anglicized Urdu accent, characterized by a mixture of English and Urdu, in which almost all of the verb and case endings are wrong. Zahra Bakhtiyar speaks English whenever possible. It is important to note that Paul only did this inconsistently in the novel, so that there are places where characters drop in and out of dialect.

All of these would be easy to capture in an Urdu text, where the appearance of non-standard Urdu would immediately signal a change into one or another of these, but they are almost completely lost when one translates into English. Incidentally, it has to be said, it is hard to imagine a person without some knowledge of English reading this novel, since so much of it is in Nastaliq English; the jarring experience of encountering English in Nastaliq in the middle of an Urdu sentence, however, was difficult to replicate in English. Wherever possible, I have tried to maintain certain signals of shifts in voice so that it can be clear that the novel was interested in these— though, indicating where the novel utilized English was nearly impossible. For instance, Bebe attempts to say the Urdu word *matlab* (meaning) but it comes out 'matbal'; the translation has her saying *neam* instead of 'mean'. The Anglo-Indian nurse says, 'Have a sheat.' In English, however, instead of sounding Anglo-Indian, sometimes she sounds drunk—an unintended consequence of a translational choice—since English has so few case and verb endings.

The other main translation problem was the number of different styles that the novel contains. It is fairly clear that Paul had cinematic aspirations for a novel like this, as much of the dialogue is written with a melodramatic Bollywood flair. But at other points, the novel has

Premchand as an inspiration: '[W]hen people are less conscious of their own beauty, they appear even more beautiful.' The aphorism as explanation for human behaviour was the hallmark of Premchand's prose. At other times, though, it is clear that Paul is in a world all his own, and remarkably, this seems to occur in the moments of Christian allegory (both with Christ and with descriptions of hell). I've attempted wherever possible to mark such moments as innovative and transformative.

This is also a novel that deals with several scientific terms that were only beginning to come into vogue in the 1960s. Wherever possible, I have tried to standardize these terms—'blood type' (instead of 'blood group'), and so on. There are other places where I have not intervened—no explanation is ever provided in the novel for the chronic blood shortage that Dr Bakhtiyar suffers from, or why he has a blood shortage but high blood pressure, and I have not tried to find one. At the same time, the word 'blood' appears more than two hundred and fifty times in the novel, and only rarely in a medical or scientific sense. More often than not 'blood' works more like a leitmotif, changing in meaning slightly, every time one encounters it.

Finally, and this bears underscoring for the non-Urdu reader, the central arc of the novel revolves around several stories from the Mahabharata. While none of the explication of the myth is ever provided in the text, it bears highlighting here, as Mohan Karan, the main character of the text, has two names from the Hindu epic—Mohan (Krishna) and Karan (Karna). If Mohan has several *gopi*s (maidens) flirting with him constantly because he is so attractive, then Karan is fated to fail because of the system that he is fighting. This mythic quality in the novel is one of the most interesting explications of the Mahabharata by changing the axis on which the main antagonists struggle.

I hope that I have done justice to a wonderful, interesting and innovative text. By highlighting my own difficulties, I hope that I have cleared a space for the true wonder of the novel to shine through.

Austin, Texas   Snehal Shingavi
December 2019

CHAPTER 1

He was strikingly handsome. Handsome, and also endearingly oblivious about his good looks. This was what caught the eye of the female receptionist at the employment exchange. She found him attractive enough to stop knitting the sweater she had been working on, and, instead, stood next to the window to the office.

She spoke to him kindly, 'I am sorry, but the last vacancy has already been filled.'

He began to turn away, dejected, but the receptionist wanted to look at him a little longer.

'You should keep in touch. I will pay special attention in case another vacancy opens up.'

'Thank you.'

As he noticed the girl looking so longingly at him, a wave of blood rushed to his pale cheeks.

Who knows what impelled the girl—

'To the left, very close by, there is a blood bank. They buy blood there. What I mean is . . .'

It was as if the girl wanted to bargain for the blood that had stalled on his face—as if she could feel his blood coursing through her own veins.

'Well, I am in desperate need of money. Please tell me the name of the blood bank.'

'People's Blood Bank.'

The girl regretted it immediately. The thought of this handsome young man's healthy blood being used for some decrepit, affluent patient had been enough perhaps to make her shudder.

'Thank you.'

As the young man turned away, the girl wanted to stop him. To invite him to meet up at the 'gay pier' that evening. But instead, she silently stared at him as he walked away.

Drip. Drip.

Two drops of water fell from the roof on to the young man's shoulder, as if the exchange building was helplessly shedding tears at its inability to offer him any assistance.

A human being encircled by flames races towards any available escape. Once he heard about the blood bank, the young man's previously dashed hopes were raised again. He located the building of the People's Blood Bank without any difficulty.

'Your name?' the elderly clerk at the blood bank asked him as he completed the entry in the register.

'Karan. M.A. Karan.'

'Karan? Very good! Are you a poet?'

'Poet? No, sir, Karan is not my pen name—it's my given name.'

'Given names are always the names of God.'

The elderly clerk seemed eager for a debate. The unexpected image of a poet friend of his, however, threw a wrench in his train of thought.

'Strange. You aren't a poet, but you are also not at all hesitant about giving blood.'

Innocently, Karan responded, 'My father—he passed away—but he used to be a very well-known poet in Hindi.'

'I see!'

The elderly clerk pretended interest and chuckled, in part at Karan's plain-spoken naivety.

'He gave blood his whole life so that he could continue writing poetry.'

'I'm glad that you are able to follow in his footsteps.'

The clerk's laughter gave his face a distorted, wizened expression.

'What I mean is, you, too, are giving blood altruistically for the betterment of people who are ill. Still, occupation?'

'I'm unemployed.'

The clerk's eyes flicked over Karan, looking him up and down, as if to say, 'I already knew that, because why else would you be here?'

'Sorry!' he said, sounding distinctly cheerful. 'Write down the addresses of all your relatives.'

'I don't have any.'

'Oh, sorry. I will just write down my address here. This is just a routine form. You need to sign here.' He extended the form towards Karan. 'Look. There is absolutely no danger involved in giving blood. The company only needs a signature as a formality. Thank you.'

Having got the form signed, the clerk rang the office bell. A servant came running in.

'Bacchu, take this man to the nurse in the operating theatre. Take his card, too.' Then, addressing the young man, he said, 'Mr Karan, first we shall determine your blood type. Each type is assigned a specific value. Bring the nurse's note with you when you return. We will determine what you are to be paid according to that.'

The Anglo-Indian nurse had just finished collecting someone else's blood in the theatre. She sat in a lounge chair, taking a drag from a cigarette, just as Bacchu arrived with Karan in tow.

'Oh . . . O!'

The nurse shook her head in exhausted frustration. But then, when she saw Karan, she couldn't stop looking at him.

'Oh! Cupid himself!' she exclaimed to herself. 'Hello!'

'Hello!' Another wave of blood washed across Karan's nervous face.

'Have a sheat.' She put out her cigarette and offered Karan a chair.

'Madam, he's here to give blood. Here is his card . . .'

'Thank you, you can go.'

Bacchu left. As Karan took his seat, the nurse went on to take out a compact from her handbag sitting on the table and applied a thin coat of fine powder to the lines on her face. Then, she redefined the outline of her lips with a light-pink lipstick. She picked up an apron, white as snow, from the hook and put it on.

'Mishter Karan,' she said, reading his name off the card. 'Pleashe roll up your left shleeve and lie down over there.' She pointed towards the bed with a flirtatious smile.

Karan silently rolled up his sleeves and went to lie down on the bed, while the nurse set up the equipment for drawing blood.

'There ish no reashon to be shcared. Why do you look sho terrified?'

'No, I am not scared . . . I . . . No . . .'

'How shweet.'

Before the next beat of her heart, she was already charmed by Karan's embarrassment.

'You are very shweet.'

As she bent to tie the tourniquet around Karan's arm, the nurse, almost deliberately, brought her right cheek as close as possible to Karan's lips, so close that they almost touched. And after tying the tourniquet, she turned her lips towards Karan's lips.

'Now open and closhe your fisht—quickly, quickly. The vein carrying your blood hash to be forced to throb.'

As he rapidly opened and closed his fist, the nurse began to search for a good vein, affectionately stroking his stiffened wrist with her hand, as if she had forgotten what she were doing altogether.

'Why are you shelling your blood?'

Karan sneaked several glances at her, but did not offer a response.

'Your own body needsh your blood.'

Karan remained silent.

'If you want to give your blood to help the poor, then donate it for free to the Red Crosh. Blood ish not shomething that should be shold.'

'My hands are tied,' admitted Karan, referring to his unemployment and poverty.

'No, your handsh are quite good and free.'

The nurse replied, completely missing Karan's point.

'You are shtrong. You can work hard and earn a living.'

For a moment, she forgot she was flirting, and began giving him advice instead.

'If you make a habit of shelling your blood for money, you will ruin your body. Why don't you work and earn a living?'

'Work?!' Karan, blurted out like an overexcited, frustrated child, choking on his own words. 'Is there any work anywhere?'

'Make an effort.'

She made that suggestion out of total ignorance.

'I've been drifting without work for years.' Karan was overcome by her sympathy. He said, 'Even if I do find an odd job here or there, they let go of me within a few days.'

'You should keep trying. Men should never give up.' For a few moments, she continued to caress Karan's wrists, and then she blurted out, 'Okay, now I will take your blood.'

She inserted the needle into one of Karan's pulsating veins, and the uncontaminated, vital blood of this starving man rose through the tube and rapidly filled the bottle. At first it was just one drop at a time, but then the drops came together in a steady flow. As the blood drained from Karan's face, it left jaundiced circles in its wake. The nurse kept staring wide-eyed at those yellowed rings. Human blood continued to flow into the bottle belonging to the People's Blood Bank.

'One pint ish more than enough.'

Impatiently, the nurse drew the needle out.

In the meantime, Bacchu returned to the theatre.

'Memsahib, shall I bring coffee for the gentleman?'

At the blood bank, every blood donor was offered a cup of coffee immediately after drawing blood.

'No, you can go.'

The nurse took a bottle of French brandy and some soda water from the cupboard and excitedly prepared two drinks. She pushed one towards Karan.

'Drink up, Mishter Karan.'

'I—I don't drink alcohol.'

'For the shake of your own blue eyesh, drink up. All of your pain will dishappear.'

Karan winced slightly, but then downed the entire drink in a single gulp.

The nurse sipped hers slowly, working on determining Karan's blood type.

'Good! Your blood is type O, RH negative. Thish ish a very rare blood type. Oh, you finished your brandy . . . here, have shome more.'

The nurse dumped another double peg into his glass.

Karan wanted to polish off the glass of brandy again.

'No. Drink it shlowly. Like me.'

'You . . . You are very kind.'

Two or three sips later, Karan began to feel tipsy.

'But, why are you making me drink alcohol?'

'Because you are very handshome.'

The nurse was overcome as she gazed deep into Karan's eyes.

'I want to shtare at you to my heart's content.'

'I don't like drinking.' Saying which, Karan brought the glass to his lips again.

'The men of your race are shtrange. Neither do they drink alcohol, nor do they openly shpeak with women. Your race—but you are very handshome. I am giving you alcohol sho that you will shtay with me a little while longer and talk to a woman like a man should.'

'I am a man. A Rajput. My uncle had a moustache thick enough to fill a fist.'

'Ish that sho!'

'Yes. After my father's death, it was uncle who took care of me. He was the one who raised me.'

As he grew increasingly intoxicated from the brandy, it soon paved the way for sad memories in Karan.

'When my uncle died . . .'

'Don't talk about death.' The nurse poured a tiny sip of brandy and said, 'Talk of death shcares me.'

She lit a cigarette. Her gaze rose along with the smoke to brush Karan's face.

'You are a Rajput?'

'Yes. I am a Rajput.'

'Are all Rajputs afraid of life?'

'No!'

Gradually, his alcohol-induced sadness disappeared and his face now sported a smile.

'Rajputs confront life head-on. You must have read about the bravery of the Rajput race in your Indian history textbooks. Maharana Pratap, Rana Sanga, Prithvi Raj Chauhan . . .'

'Kissh me if you are sho brave.'

'What? Me . . . you . . .?' Karan was dumbstruck. 'Why are you looking at me like that?'

The nurse began to laugh.

'Dear boy, you may very well be a Rajput, but you may ash well alsho be a giant piece of toffee.'

As she tossed back her short, untied hair, she took on a seductive air.

'Okay, sho tell me—how do I look?'

'Very lovely! If I can find a decent job, I would certainly marry you.'

'Marry?'

Karan's innocence amused the nurse.

'You will marry me? Oh . . . How naughty!'

'Yes, marry! I will definitely marry you. Rajput men only kiss women after they marry them. I will also marry that girl from the Employment Exchange. I will marry all the girls. I quite like girls . . .'

'And girls sheem to like you . . . Here, take your chit. Give it to the clerk and collect the money for your blood.'

Karan took the chit.

'You didn't even ashk for my name? What kind of boyfriend are you?'

'Your name is Woman.'

'No, my name is Bele Rina.'

'Bele Rina! Bele Rina is a very beautiful name. Goodbye, Bele Rina!'

'. . . Bye! Will you come and shee me?'

'Yes. I will definitely see you again. If I can't find work, I will at least be back to give more blood.'

'No! No!' Bele Rina was laughing so hard that she felt as if her eyes were swimming in tears.

Karan left, exiting the theatre, headed in the direction of the elderly clerk's office.

'Bacchu says that the nurse is quite fond of you,' the clerk said as he laughed.

'Yes.' Karan was trying to regain control of his senses as the intoxication from the brandy swept over him. 'I just gave her my blood. Here, take my chit.'

The clerk took the chit.

'This is a rare blood type. A pint of this fetches forty rupees here. Here is your payment.'

As he took the money for his blood, Karan felt like a wild animal, crazed from hunger, gnawing at its own flesh, beginning to consume it.

'You should take these forty rupees and make another pint of blood. Then you can make another forty rupees. Your blood is quite rare.'

Karan wadded up the notes and put them in his pocket.

'You should consider yourself very lucky. I work myself to the bone at this place every month in order to make a meagre one hundred and fifty rupees.'

'At least you earn your living. All I did was give blood.'

The world-weary clerk muffled a chuckle.

'You may very well be your father's dream come to life, but you are terribly naive. My dear brother, every poor man gives his blood to make a living. Some, like you, by sticking a needle in their veins, and some, like me, by breaking their backs day after day . . . In both cases, the master demands his full pint of blood . . . Well, right now you seem a little drunk. We can finish this conversation next time. When the money runs out, don't hesitate to come back.'

'Thank you!'

'For what? You are getting paid for your own blood, after all. The truth is, we are supposed to take blood from an individual only once every three months. But, sometimes we do take blood without entering it into the register, if a donor is in need of money. Well then, goodbye!'

As he exited the gate of the blood bank, Karan put his right hand in the pocket of his trousers. When his fingers touched the forty rupees, he felt as if the bottle of brandy had reappeared, dressed in Bele Rina's clothes, with painted lips that forced themselves on to the lips of the Rajput. The Rajput couldn't help smiling.

On his way, Karan spotted a friend, whom he owed five rupees to.

'Akbar!'

Akbar, in his turn, quickened his pace trying to disappear into the crowd. Perhaps the poor man was afraid that Karan was after some more money.

'Akbar!'

Karan ran to catch up to him and when he finally did, he took Akbar's hand in his own and held on warmly.

'I have an important thing to take care of, Karan.'

'Here are the five rupees I owe you, my friend. And if your business isn't pressing, come with me to a restaurant. You are a true friend. We can at least have some tea together. Today I don't even care if you drink my blood. Come!'

'No, I should go.'

Placing the five-rupee note safely in his pocket, Akbar looked at Karan with some surprise.

'You seem to be in good spirits, my friend. How did you get so tipsy?'

'Bele Rina is a wonderful girl, Akbar. I can only offer you tea, Akbar, or perhaps my blood. But if you want to drink liquor, I can take you to see Bele Rina.'

'Who is Bele Rina?'

'Bele Rina is a woman. A goddess! I worship Bele Rina . . .'

Karan's eyes lit up at the thought of the nurse.

Akbar was anxious that Karan might become even more melodramatic, and they were in a public place.

'Okay, my friend, I am going.'

'Okay. Goodbye . . .'

For a long while, Karan wandered hither and thither on the streets, warmly greeting every casual acquaintance he ran into. The weight of the money in his pocket gave his fluttering heart the ability to lift the human veil that separated him from the rest of humanity. He felt an intense desire to love everyone, secretly, in his intoxication, to embrace even his own desperate hunger.

'Bhaiyaji, I touch your feet.'

Eventually, even after the intoxication from the brandy had worn off, his mind continued to laugh and play in the fog.

'May you have a long life, my son. Tell me, did you find any work?'

'I am bound to find something soon, Bhaiyaji.'

He was trying to convince himself with his own sincerity.

'Tell me, how is Didi?'

'She is very ill, son. Her health will improve, but it will be a gradual process.'

'Yes, Bhaiyaji. She will definitely get better. Bad days don't last forever.'

Without thinking, he put his hand in his pocket, and as he caressed the notes, he said to himself: 'I, too, will definitely find a job.'

Once he had left, Bhaiyaji said to his companion: 'He's a very good lad. He lives with an elderly widow in our neighbourhood. The unfortunate woman is all alone and she is very poor, but the lowliest people always have the biggest hearts.'

As he passed by a clothier's shop, Karan imagined the face of the old woman. From beneath her dirty, tattered, and torn dupatta peeked a face of compassion mixed in a mesh of wrinkles. He had never seen Bebe wearing a proper dupatta.

'I need white muslin, for a dupatta.'

'Two and a half yards—four and a half rupees.'

As he handed the money to the shopkeeper, Karan wondered how Bebe would look in this pristine, clean dupatta. How excited she would be. He felt as happy as if his own mother was adorned in a dupatta he had bought for her.

'May you have a long life, my dearest, my moon, my sun . . .' she would bless him with joy and pride.

'What did my mother look like? What was she like? She would have taken me in her lap and kissed me over and over . . .' Orphaned children spend their whole lives trying to keep a place open in their hearts, a place that holds the imagined faces of their mothers and fathers.

'Karne, my son.' The elderly widow had recognized Karan's pain and tried to console him. 'Those who have no one have God.'

'But Bebe, sometimes I want God to transform into my mother—at least then I would be able to know what my mother looked like.'

'Shall I show you some ready-made shirts?' The shopkeeper, noticing Karan's threadbare clothes, offered.

'Yes . . .' Capriciously, Karan grew excited at first, but soon came to his senses. He was worried about the unnecessary expense. 'No . . .'

As he left the clothier's shop, he spied a child crying by the side of the street, and stopped.

'Are you looking for your mother?'

'No, I am hungry—Mother asked me to go and beg for your food.'

'Oh . . .'

As Karan took two annas from his pocket and placed it in the child's hand, he also realized that he should avoid spending any more money. As soon as he arrived home, he would give the entire amount to Bebe. He didn't want Bebe's love to forget its lullabies and turn into reprimands and rebukes.

Finally, through a narrow and dingy alley where he quickened his pace, Karan arrived at the front door of his house.

'Bebe!'

Knocking on the locked door, his eyes were fixed on
the new dupatta for the old woman.

'Bebe!'

'Bebe is at Ramjas's house.' The window of the house
facing his was open, and then Ragini, the young wife
of the elderly Hakeem Sukh Chen, had hung her arm,
decked out with multicoloured bangles, out the window.
She smiled at him saying, 'Here, take the key.'

'Oh right, I didn't notice the lock on the door.'

As he took the key, Karan's hand lingered on Ragini's
finger, and her pretty smile turned into a laugh. Her
silken dupatta slid off her head and fell below her chest.
Her heavy breathing made her studded necklace swing
and sparkle. She winked mischievously.

'Khoo khoo khaa khaa!' Sukh Chen, the elderly
Hakeem, coughed, and shattered Karan's lovely moment.

'He, he, he he, he!' Ragini's laughter tinkled, like
a beautiful, nuanced, longed-for melody, created by
a maestro on the sitar.

'The elderly Hakeem's Bele Rina is really very
enticing,' Karan thought to himself.

'You should at least have a taste,' Ragini's eyes called
out to him flirtatiously.

'I am always dangling near your lips like an orange.'

After his daring confessions to Bele Rina, Karan
now fancied himself close to everyone. With every
fibre of his being, he cursed Professor Hari Singh
Rajput for not being able to kiss Bele Rina's lips even
when drunk. For, it was in the Professor's history texts

that he had read unrelenting praises of Rajput ethics over and over again.

'You never even look at me,' Ragini complained, staring into Karan's blue eyes with deep longing.

Karan took her hand with the jingling, multicoloured bangles, and pressed it in his own.

But, immediately spotting a man approaching from a distance, Karan turned his back to Ragini and began to open the door to his house. Once inside his room, he opened the window that looked out on the alley and hummed a song from a film. He could have replaced just any film actor crooning promises of love to Hakeem Sukh Chen's wife.

'Let us go-o-o!'

Puran Singh, the street peddler, came through the alley announcing his presence. The Hakeem's wife hid partially behind the curtain.

'Wait!' Karan called out to Puran Singh. He stepped out to buy two loaves of bread and some chickpea curry from the vendor, before heading back inside. He then sat down on the charpoy in front of the window to eat.

The chickpea curry was so spicy that his breathing grew heavy. He glanced over at the Hakeem's window where Ragini was sitting on a tall stool made of reeds gazing out in his direction. She appealed to him like a full pot of sweet lassi.

'Khoo . . . khoo . . . khaa . . . khaa . . . kho!'

The full pot of sweet lassi was once again dashed to pieces. The hand with the multicoloured bangles quickly closed the window as Hakeem Sukh Chen walked up to his house and turned to look at Karan's open one, coughing angrily.

CHAPTER 2

The following morning, Karan spent quite some time just tossing and turning in his bed.

Bebe, wearing the new dupatta he had purchased, was making him tea.

'Karne, O Karne, my child!'

Karan rubbed his eyes and sat up in bed, looking at the woman in the courtyard outside.

'Get up, son. Drink your tea. If I am late getting to work, Ramjas's wife will be furious.'

Her face, wrapped in the plain dupatta, carried a glow of new strength.

Karan got out of bed quickly, to get ready.

'Bebe, Ramjas's wife bullies you all the time.'

'What can I say, son, she is a tyrant.'

'You should stop working there, Bebe.'

As soon as he had said this though, he realized his error and changed the emphasis of his comment. 'What I mean is, as soon as I get a job, you should stop working there.'

'Of course, son. Once you get a job, what will there be to worry about?'

'Bebe!' Ragini's voice filtered in, and then, Ragini herself appeared at the courtyard, following her own voice. 'I have brought you some halwa.'

For the past several days, she had been very affectionate with Bebe.

Karan was sitting behind Bebe rinsing out his mouth. He lifted his gaze to look at Ragini and was immediately transfixed. She was particularly made up today. Flowers adorned her hair, and her head was raised like the hood of a cobra's, holding one's gaze hypnotically. She had adorned her delicate earlobes with quivering, sparkling, dangling earrings. A yellow, silken dupatta with a filigreed border housed a thick braid, which suddenly snaked its way out, and her perfectly round face looked flushed with a deep red rouge.

To Karan it seemed as if the morning sun had overlooked Hakeem Sukh Chen's high balcony and entered his courtyard instead.

'The Hakeem has just left for his shop. I thought that since the halwa was warm and fresh, I would bring some over.'

'That is very kind of you.'

Karan, who was washing his face with an Indian-made soap that was so crude and rough that it was used to wash clothes, laughed out loud.

'Daughter, this brother-in-law of yours is very mischievous.' The old woman's experienced eyes surmised Ragini's desires.

After all, if one could happily enjoy halwa in one's own imagination, then what was the point of jealously watching others eat halwa?

'Daughter, do you know what Karne did yesterday?'

Ragini looked confused from head to toe.

'Yesterday, he sold his blood and bought this dupatta of mine. A full half kilo of blood!'

'Dear God!' The new bride's hair ornament shuddered and fell across her face.

'I put the remaining money in my blouse. Even in these dark times, who would dare to pawn such precious things?'

The border of the old woman's clean dupatta darkened as she wiped away her tears.

'He should only ever have to sell the blood of his enemies. Ask me for whatever money you might need, Bebe.'

Karan wiped his face with a dirty towel and smiled. He looked in her direction charmingly.

'Take this ten-rupee note, Bebe.'

She put a finger inside the brassiere under her fancy kameez, took out a note, and handed it to Bebe.

'Make him drink very warm milk every morning. If a man loses even an ounce of blood he becomes half-dead. Half a kilo of blood—dear God!'

Terrified, she placed a finger on a vein near his palm.

'May you live a long life, son.'

As she tied the note up in her pallu, the old woman was reminded of her daughter, Lubhai, whom Prabhu Dayal Moncho Walla would visit their home daily and find some excuse to put a few rupees in the old woman's bag.

'What's the big deal if Ragini wants to visit? Lubhai is now the mother of five children, and she happily rules her household. I would hardly let anything happen to her honour.' She consoled herself as she tightly held the note wrapped in her pallu inside her fist.

'Difficult times have to be endured some way or another.'

'Daughter, I have raised him as if he were my own son. But he never listens to me. He might listen to you . . .'

Ragini completely forgot about Hakeem Sukh Chen and blushed as if Karan were helping her down from her bridal palanquin and bringing her home.

'What I mean is . . .' The old woman was reminded of having to scrub clean Ramjas's dirty dishes till the faded patterns on them were revealed. 'A brother-in-law and a sister-in-law are not strangers to one another. You need to make him understand that he should never go and give his blood away. I spit at money earned this way.'

'Bebe,' Karan came and sat near them once he was finished getting ready, 'if poor people like us don't give our blood, then some other poor, sick person will suffer until he dies. Just think, Bebe, drops of my blood could save someone from death.'

Karan had hoped to sound sincere, but his words had failed to convince even himself.

'Son, even an uneducated person like me knows this.'

Without much thought, the old woman tossed the note that was wrapped in her pallu behind her, and suddenly, the grace of some angel descended upon her toothless face.

'It is our duty to give blood to a dying man. But it is also a sin to sell blood, my son. You didn't donate blood for a cause, darling, you traded your blood to earn money for food. This is hardly doing a good deed. It's desperation. The people who bought your blood will make ten times the amount they gave you. Just look at your face. It looks like the pale moon that you see during the day.'

Ragini lifted her head and looked over at Karan, as if to say, 'I think that the moon looks sallow even in the dark of night.'

'Why did you need to bring this old woman this shroud?' she said pointing at her new dupatta. Her heart really did well up then, two teardrops, like pearls, glimmering in her eyes.

'I can bear Ramjas's orders, son. I can deal with the criticisms of my daughters and sons-in-law, but I will never agree to leaving this house. You tell me, daughter, had I a son of my own, would I ever accept money earned in exchange for his blood?'

Karan touched the old woman's feet.

'I am your son, too, Bebe. You are my mother.'

'Then never go to give your blood to these villains ever again.'

'No, Bebe, there's no more reason for me to go there. I will find work soon. There is a girl in the employment agency. She said she would help me.'

At the mention of a girl, Ragini's ears perked up.

'First take care of your health, then you can worry about getting a job!'

Ragini's jealous admonition reminded the old woman of the ten-rupee note tied up in her pallu dangling behind her. She immediately wrapped her fist around the knot of her pallu.

'I am getting late for Ramjas's house. I have left a glass of tea for you. You should also have some of Daughter's halwa.'

'I should go, too, Bebe.'

When the old woman and Ragini had left, Karan found himself alone in the courtyard. At first he was tempted to open the window facing the lane and call Ragini back. But he decided against it and turned back after having walked a few steps towards the window.

He was so ravenous that the white teardrop-shaped almonds that adorned the halwa seemed like the beautiful teeth of Lord Indra's apsaras, openly displayed, beginning to speak. 'Look at us first. Nourish yourself well and then you can think about your Ragini. Ragini, on a full stomach, would be much more beautiful.'

And as Karan slowly chewed and relished the almonds that were soaked in the sweetness of the lovely, warm halwa, he was reminded of all the possible pleasures of work and employment. The halwa was soon finished.

And then he licked his fingers and turned towards the glass of tea.

'What image of Ragini can I find in this?' he wondered.

The beautiful shoes locked away in a wedding trousseau always long for someone to open the trousseau and embrace them—and I am at no fault, staring at the wondrous trunk of a spring wedding, slowing losing all control of myself . . . khaa . . . khaa . . . khoo . . . khoo . . . and Hakeem Sukh Chen is also at no fault, who coughs in such fury that makes him cough even more.

Karan heard a gentle knock on the door, the sound penetrating his thoughts.

His hunger was completely satiated, and with a satisfied belch, he got up to open the door.

Outside, he found Ragini waiting, and looking at her, he felt like countless, rapid melodies burst forth from every point on her body, sending tremors into this sleepy alley.

'I have brought some sweets made from melon seeds for you. Hakeemji made them himself with his own hands.'

The alley began to wake up to the loud notes of Ragini's voice. Karan quickly pulled the Hakeem's wife inside and bolted the door.

CHAPTER 3

An illicit relationship, unlike the legitimate relationship of husband and wife, could burn out like dying embers. Ragini's desire was more rationality than love, and that's why, Karan and Ragini's feelings could not last longer than a few days or weeks.

Karan began to feel the weight of social stigma.

Moreover, he began to despise himself for living off of Ragini's scraps. But neither did he stop living off of them, nor he did not stop despising himself. He was like a prostitute who adorned her bed while cursing her client, but still waited in anticipation for him to arrive.

On most days, after his morning tea, Karan left home to wander aimlessly for an hour or two. By the time Bebe left for work, he returned, and spent the rest of morning stretched out on the bed, reading provocative mystery and romance novels.

In the meantime, Ragini would be busy with wrapping up Hakeemji's household tasks, and once her chores were done, she arrived at Karan's door with either halwa or yogurt and parathas.

Before her arrival, the door remained closed but not latched. Once safely inside, she latched the door and went on to stand at the foot of Karan's bed. Without even thinking, his wounded pride playing constantly in his mind, Karan spread out his arms to the side. Had Karan even laid there disinterestedly, Ragini would not have got upset. The two of them, with their desires fully sated, tried to placate each other with lifeless smiles.

Ragini's response was no longer a sweet melody for Karan. In its place, Karan imagined a child wailing in Ragini's arm, as the stench of the child's urine wafted from Ragini's clothes. And instead of trying to make love to Karan, it seemed as if she was trying to quiet the child down with both threats and caresses.

'Can I tell you something?' she said to Karan, one day, uncharacteristically angrily.

'What—?'

'My feet are swollen.'

When the young wife of a well-to-do, elderly husband is about to become the mother of a child, she sits down on some ancient hill, full of contentment, and falls asleep, like when the older wife of a poor, young husband catches wind of his earnings and suddenly rediscovers her youthfulness.

'You . . .?'

'Yes. I'm pregnant.'

Ragini wrapped her entire head in a dupatta, like Bebe did.

'Khaa . . . khaa . . . khoo!'

Karan unconsciously began coughing like Hakeem Sukh Chen.

It had been a long time since Ragini looked at him this way, with pride and love.

Karan felt as though hellish forces were punishing him for his crimes and had turned him into a child, hanging upside down in Ragini's womb.

He found it difficult to breathe.

'He is very happy.'

'Who?'

Karan was still looking for opportunities to humiliate Hakeem Sukh Chen.

'Arré! Hakeemji . . . who else?'

'Is he happy because his wife is going to be the mother of another man's child?'

'You are being unnecessarily sarcastic. That poor man is like a cow, sacred to God. What could he possibly know of our deceptions?'

'Of course. I am the one who is Satan's instrument.'

Karan became upset.

'What are you arguing about?'

Ragini pushed back a lock of hair that had fallen across Karan's face as if he were her own infant child.

'How could a man possibly bear the thought of his woman rearing a bastard in her womb?'

'But whenever he looks at me, he does cough angrily. He was suspicious at first, but I have smoothed everything over.'

'As your child gets older, he will call Hakeemji "Father".'

'Well, there isn't any other option, is there? Should he call you "Father" instead?'

The words burst forth from Ragini's lips involuntarily, and realizing her mistake, she quickly tried to remedy things: 'What is the child's fault in all of this, what is mine? This is the way the world works. You might be the real father, but only the *father* can be the father.'

'Yes, yes. You are right, of course. Your Hakeem is like my father, too, since I eat from the money that he provides.'

Karan suddenly recalled the day he sold his blood and thought to himself, 'Ragini has also profited from my blood so that her wealthy husband would not die without an heir.'

'Okay, let's drop this. Eat this carrot halwa. It turned out quite delicious.'

As he ate the sweet carrot halwa, the bitterness of apprehension coated Karan's tongue.

'Nature has gifted women with a very profound understanding. No matter her age, she always appears innocent and oppressed, but ultimately, at every age, she gets the exact outcome that she desires, and in every situation, she even finds a moral justification for her every move.'

This new-found formality between Karan and Ragini was increasing with each passing day. She rarely even appeared pleased to see Karan any more. Once, when they ran into each other, Ragini acted like Karan was a stranger.

'The poor Hakeem is still completely clueless. Ever since he learnt that I was pregnant, he comes home four times a day,' she said. Ragini seemed very content with the fact that her husband kept such a close eye on her. 'Now you tell me, if he comes home while I am here, our secret will be out and he will be extremely hurt.'

Even though Karan had lost interest in her, he boiled over like a hot cauldron when he heard this. Ragini placed her hands on her belly, to protect her husband's treasure from a stranger.

That very morning, Ragini, filled with great devotion, had gone to hear the pandit at the Chowk Mandir recite a moral tale. In the story, a faithful, married woman made a wooden idol of her husband after he had died. She would tell all of her friends, 'Sister, does it matter whether a husband is made of wood or not?'

'My husband is a living, breathing idol.'

When she recalled this, Ragini looked away from Karan. In her mind, she placed a spittoon in front of her husband's coughing face, as she slowly massaged his chest. She felt a sense of peace at this thought of serving him.

In the earlier days, when she was on her way to see Karan, she would race over to him, insensate, compulsive.

A man dying of thirst will even cut across fire in order to get to a well. But once his thirst is quenched, he sits in a safe corner somewhere to reflect on his fearlessness, and is stupefied.

Ragini was also bewildered that she had actually done all that she had. She now regarded her about-to-be-born child as her husband's. Her narrow outlook on life was not prepared to acknowledge any other possibilities about its pedigree.

But the married woman inside of her tried to convince herself that there was no problem here. A child always belongs to its father, the one with whom a bride, draped in her red wedding shawl, circles the wedding fire.

A house that was filled, a husband that fulfilled her every desire, with only the absence of a child in her lap, and even that matter would be settled within a few days.

In this state, imagining complete security and peace, if Ragini feared anything, it was that someone had caught wind of her relationship with Karan.

The funny thing about suspicion is that it grows in the mind of the one who is most likely guilty, before it even occurs to others. One can say that the suspicion directed at someone else is, in fact, the echo of one's own terror and guilt.

'O Sister Bhagwati, I've heard that this Karna is causing quite a commotion in his neighbourhood.' Ragini's heart skipped a beat. She eavesdropped, from her doorstep, on the conversation of the two older women.

'Why are you blaming Karne? When a woman has lost all sense of shame then what is the man's fault? They are, after all, just like horses.'

'Oh, so it's Ragini's fault for ruining him?'

'Who can ruin a man? In the end, it is always the woman who is ruined, Dayawanti.'

'You are right, sister. But what can I say? That poor woman is also blameless.'

'Yes, you know what it is about people? They take insignificant matters and start taking aim at people needlessly.'

'The poor woman spends all her time serving her husband. What else was she supposed to do?'

'I hear she is pregnant.'

'Really?'

Ragini stepped out of her doorway like the epitome of a good wife, Sita, and drove her gaze into the ground.

'I touch your feet, aunt. I also touch your feet, aunt.'

She folded her hands respectfully as if she had just suddenly come upon the two aunts.

'May you be bathed in milk, may you be blessed with children, may you have a long, married life.'

The two crones simultaneously offered their series of blessings.

'Where are you going, daughter?'

'To get bread, aunt,' Ragini responded. 'He will be home soon. At this hour, he only takes his milk with bread.'

'How far along is your pregnancy?'

Her aunt's curiosity poked and prodded her until she spilt forth.

'I'm in my third month, aunt.'

'Good. May God bring the happy occasion soon. The Hakeem has been dying for the sight of a child.'

Ragini tried to look embarrassed.

'She is such a good woman,' the aunt said after she had walked on.

'Yes, did you notice? She never lifted her gaze from the ground.'

'People say such nonsensical things.'

'True. What can you say about most people? They wouldn't even hesitate to raise criticisms of Sati Sita!'

After that incident, Ragini never saw Karan again.

One morning, as she was leaving for work at Ramjas's house, Bebe noticed Karan still tossing around in his bed.

'Karne, get up, son. You've overslept.'

'Yes, Bebe.' Karan yawned as he rubbed his eyes.

'Have you heard, Karne? The Hakeem's wife is going to her mother's home.'

As was her habit, she washed and scrubbed her words just like she did with Ramjas's soiled clothes.

'She will have her child there, too. She will stay there for at least six months to a year.'

Karan listened quietly.

'You are young, you should be enjoying yourself, but the elders weren't wrong in their advice, either. Eat, but also leave a trail of crumbs. A man who looks ahead and behind him as he walks, never gets lost.'

'I don't understand what you are trying to say, Bebe.'

'What I *neam*, my son, is that you need to concern yourself with finding a job. You need to have some way to earn a living.'

Once Bebe left, instead of feeling angry with Ragini, Karan felt sorry for himself.

The truth was that he was certain that he wanted to end things with Ragini, but he couldn't bring himself to do it. And he knew that the reason for his silence was his hunger and his poverty. So despite his disinterest, he let the affair go on. But when he saw Ragini avoiding him, it hurt his pride.

A little later, Karan got ready to leave home. At the door, he saw Hakeem Sukh Chen running as fast as he could ahead of his wife. Ragini had come to drop him off at the threshold of their home.

'Khaa . . . khoo!'

The Hakeem coughed, briefly, as he turned towards Karan.

'Namaste, Karanji.'

The Hakeem's tone was exceedingly cheerful.

'Namaste, ji.'

'Found any work yet?'

'No.'

Karan did not have to look at Ragini's face to guess that she was smiling beneath her show of concern for his plight.

CHAPTER 4

Suicide, whether considered in the abstract or the concrete, was eventually undone for the coward by the power of its internal contradictions. But succumbing to one's internal conflicts was itself a sign of cowardice. A coward is even too terrified of a quick suicide, something like burning himself alive or placing his neck across a train track. Instead, he prefers those forms of suicide in which life gradually leaves the body over a long stretch of time. And with it, the delusion that was life could dissipate proportionally.

Karan was beginning to find the trials of his own life so spirit-obliterating that he constantly dreamt of ways to end it. When the heart seems to stop at every beat, it was better for it to stop all together. However, despite his fantasies of dying, Karan was very afraid of death. He was so much the coward that once, after he hung a noose in his room, he quickly removed it as he shuddered at the possibility of death. What he really wanted was to remain unaware while death wore away at his walls surreptitiously. He wished death would just break in and rob him blind, without arousing the slightest of suspicion.

Ragini went home to her parents. This, Bebe believed, was the reason that Karan was sad and depressed all the time.

'My child, why are you making yourself sick? There are thousands of girls out there. And marriage isn't far off. All that we need now is for you to get your hands on a steady job.'

When the wounds of depression run deep, words of consolation are seldom appreciated.

'And remember, don't you ever go back to those damned blood dealers again.'

But Karan believed that, in her own way, Bebe was reminding him of that option. In his head, Bebe's words sounded a bit different: 'Go and give blood once more. You won't die from giving a few more drops of blood. We have to keep the house running, don't we?'

'What was the point of the blood made from Ragini's halwa and parathas, anyway? In truth, it is best if it were to be purged from my body,' he thought as he agreed with his version of Bebe's proposal.

He had made up his mind that giving his blood was the best move. He took his wrist in his hand and imagined, wide-eyed, watching his blood course.

'I am definitely going there. I will go one more time, just one more time.'

Absorbed in his bitter thoughts, he headed towards the People's Blood Bank.

'Your body needs your own blood.' Bele Rina's touching words, long trapped in his memory, suddenly burst forth.

'Bele Rina! Bele Rina!' Like some nineteenth-century English Romantic poet, Karan lost himself in a portrait of Bele Rina.

Despite being a working woman, Bele Rina was not what people derisively called a 'working girl'. She possessed a tremendous amount of womanly emotion. Even while taking someone's blood, her earnest eyes welled up with tears. She wore a yellowish powder because her heart was dejected. She drank brandy so that her mind could escape the shadows of death, so she could laugh and lighten the weight of others' troubles. And intoxicated, she did kind things for others—talking incessantly to them, as her bounty of words made the layers of lipstick on her lips disappear.

'Bele Rina!' Karan called out for her as if he had just been bitten by a cobra and Bele Rina were some sympathetic snake-charmer, lowering her head to suck the poison out of his body. But he stopped the snake-charmer's head.

'No! No! Your blood is filled with poison. I will shuck out all of your poison. I will make your body very healthy again.'

'My body is not a body, Bele Rina. It's a bottle, filled with blood, for sale.'

'No!' Bele Rina's voice seemed to drip with tears and she removed the guise of the snake-charmer and brought forth a bottle of brandy.

'Your body is the body of the shon of man.'

'The body of the poor can never house the spirit of man.' Karan was in the mood for a rousing debate. 'Rather, the rich use him like their own property.'

'No!' Bele Rina wanted to silence him with her screams.

'I need money, and for that, I will sell my blood, Bele Rina. Sell my thoughts. Sell my soul. You, yourself, play with snakes because you need money. Like me, you, too, have sold your thoughts, soul, blood, all—to those serpents. Your body is not a home for your soul, but a trivial part of the blood bank's furniture.'

Confounded, Bele Rina brought the bottle of brandy to her lips.

'Bele Rina, if you were your own master, you wouldn't trade in your virtue and your values. You would have contempt for the People's Blood Bank and would volunteer for the survival of humanity with the Red Cross's free blood-bank service.'

Bele Rina swallowed a mouthful of brandy and interrupted him, 'Your race has no idea how to have a convershation. You always make these long shpeechesh. Here, drink thish brandy.'

'Wait, Bele Rina. Let me first finish what I am trying to say. What I want to tell you is that we all put a price on our virtue, and by doing so, we become helpless.

If we don't, our virtue goes mad from hunger and runs off on its own. It is better to sell our virtue to Satan than to watch it starve to death.'

'Brandy! Drink the brandy!'

And Karan imagined himself drinking a shot of brandy. He had thought that when he would see Bele Rina today, he wouldn't bore her with his meaningless blather, but rather start a conversation about the future of Anglo-Indians in India. And then, she would offer him some brandy. And if she didn't, he would ask for some. After having had some brandy, he would kiss her lips without her permission, and . . . and . . .

But he took his wild imaginings by the collar and shook them.

'The manners of women have confounded and unmanned me. I can smell the potent perfume of Ragini's body on every woman. Bele Rina is not Ragini. The scent from Bele Rina's body is different somehow.'

Finally, he arrived at the porch of the People's Blood Bank and stopped. He found himself staring at the back of an ambulance, standing under the porch, with a giant red cross on it. He wanted to turn away from it but, helplessly, he kept on staring.

As he continued to stare, he was taken with an unshakeable curiosity, as if his own blood, from head to toe, had begun to pulse with a singular question.

'Two thousand years ago . . .'

Karan's thoughts were speaking to him again.

'. . . that heavy cross was tied to the shoulders and arms of some virtuous human being and then, he was whipped repeatedly and made to walk miles barefoot through the public markets. Then in some square, nails were driven through the palms of that honest, virtuous human and into that cross, and the heavy wood of that cross was drenched red, inside and out, with the sacred blood of that incomparable human being. The sacrifice of that great man is still alive today, even after two thousand years. His blood has become immortal!'

Karan's own blood appeared afflicted to him.

'But why, in this age, do the priests of gold tell every poor man that he is as great as Christ? Why have they hammered nails and attached the cross to every single poor person? Why do the poor have to suffer the same, relentless anguish that uniquely belongs to God's own son?' Karan became exceedingly troubled at this thought.

'If every poor person has to be tied to a cross then why does the colour of his blood fade? Why doesn't he receive infinite credit for his sacrifice? Why are the doors of sainthood and immortality closed to him?'

After a few moments, a nurse with the Red Cross walked out in a hurry from the People's Blood Bank building and got into the ambulance. Even after the ambulance had departed, Karan could still see the red cross in his mind's eye.

'Hello!' The elderly clerk from the People's Blood Bank, who had stopped at the doorway, called out to Karan.

'Have you come to give blood? . . . Hello?'

Karan looked at him as if he was coming out of a trance.

'Oh . . . hello!'

As soon as he got his bearings and recognized the clerk, Karan's voice took on the warmth of familiarity.

The two of them continued talking as they went inside the blood bank.

'You will have to wait a little while,' the elderly clerk explained to him as he entered his office. 'Two men are giving blood in the theatre right now.'

He sat down on his chair and offered Karan a seat in front of him.

'What's the matter? You look just as unsettled as my boss. And just like him, you don't seem well. You haven't started needing blood instead of giving it, have you?' he spoke in a matter-of-fact tone.

'How could a poor man take someone else's blood, Shree . . .?'

'Acharya,' the clerk offered his name.

'Shree Acharyaji. A poor man can't even claim his own blood as his own.'

'Come now, if your blood wasn't your own, you should have handed the money over to me instead of taking it yourself.'

Acharya opened the registry and began entering Karan's details.

'It's taken you a while to return, hasn't it? You haven't found work, have you?'

'If I had found work, I wouldn't come here now, would I?'

But Karan knew that was not true; he certainly would have returned to see Bele Rina. He wanted to ask Acharya about her . . . but he kept silent.

'Hmm. Yes. Mm-hmm . . . You may not realize, my friend, that there are several people who come here even after they have found work. Look at this waiting list—at least thirty per cent of these people are employed.'

Karan looked up from the list and stared at Acharya quizzically.

'Brother, these days an employed person has to earn enough to feed ten or more unemployed people. What are the poor wretches to do other than sell their own blood? But we cannot give every one of these a chance straight away. We have most of their blood types in excess quantities lying useless in storage.'

'Acharyaji, human blood can never be useless. The people whose blood fills your bottles have given so much blood that their bodies have now become broken and lifeless, like that of an ass.'

'And yet, they still keep waiting for their opportunity. You, however, are quite fortunate. Your blood type is extremely rare. We would have sent people out to look for you had you not come back in a few more days. Where have you been all this time?'

'Running away from myself. And when I finally found myself, I came to you to give blood,' Karan replied.

'You've become quite the philosopher, my friend. That's one definite benefit to being plagued by this damned unemployment. A man finds quite a bit of time to read and think. You seemed a bit naive the last time around.'

'Acharyaji, only a well-to-do man could afford naivety and other such luxuries. These qualities can be quite expensive.'

'Well said! You've really become quite wise of late. Here, take a cigarette . . .' Acharya said as he lit one for himself.

'No, I don't smoke.'

'Of course, friend, why would you accept a disgusting cigarette from a poor man like me. It's not as though it is Bele Rina's brandy. But my friend, she doesn't work here any more.'

'Oh, then where?'

'Hmm. Mm-hmm. Yes. Hmm. I got a real kick out of seeing you squirm. Youth, you know. Spring arrives and even the hungry are moved to excitement. I was young once, too. Who cared if I didn't earn enough to eat . . . I was happy spending my days chasing after girls.'

Acharya lost himself in his reminiscences about his younger days.

'Come, friend, have a smoke.'

At Acharya's insistence, Karan lit a cigarette, and immediately succumbed to rattling coughs.

'Mr Karan, take slow puffs. At the beginning of each intoxication, one must start slowly. You young people prefer everything fast these days. This is why you lose your breath so quickly.'

'Where did Bele Rina go?' It was as if Karan were searching for a dream that had been lost for a long time.

'I don't know where she went. I told the boss that he should do whatever it takes to keep her on.'

Once he had entered his details into the register, Acharya gave Karan a 'risk form' to sign.

'Young men come the first time to give blood, but the second time, the blood is an excuse to see her. Thank you,' he said as he took back the signed risk form.

'That woman was quite enticing but she was also quite emotional. Last month, a feeble, old man came to give blood. He also had a rare blood type and we had been in desperate need of it for a long-standing client. But Bele Rina was dead set against taking his blood.'

Karan put out his cigarette and started concentrating deeply on Acharya's narrative.

'When the boss tried to threaten her, that foolish girl tendered her resignation saying that she wouldn't turn the old man's blood into soup just so we could eat. She said she would join the Red Cross to atone for the sins of her past. She was convinced she would spend the rest of her life helping the poor.'

Karan breathed a sigh of contentment. To him, it felt as if Bele Rina had left the People's Blood Bank only to move into his heart, as she descended into one of its secret chambers.

'Bele Rina did the right thing, Acharyaji, in answering the call of humanity. At the Red Cross, Bele Rina's service will be directed to those who are actually in need. They don't buy and sell blood over there. They take spare blood for free and distribute it to those who need it.'

'Only rubbish is given away for free.' Acharya removed his spectacles and placed them on the table.

'What kind of person goes there to give blood anyway? Why aren't you there right now? The Red Cross's blood bank is always empty. The nun who just came in the ambulance purchased some blood for some patient of hers and left.'

Acharya picked up his spectacles and put them on.

'My young friend, if you think that buying and selling food is a legitimate business, then so is buying and selling blood.'

Karan was tempted to retort with, 'Acharyaji, I won't sell my blood here. I am going to the Red Cross's blood bank. I will donate my blood to them for free. Bele Rina has opened my eyes.'

But at that moment, all he could hear was Bebe's voice saying, 'You have to find some way to earn a living, Karne.'

He remained silent.

'I know you are not so foolish,' Acharya said, reading his mind, 'as to give your blood away for free. Such charitable ideas can only be dreamt up by those who have excessive amounts of idle wealth. You yourself, however, are poor.'

Karan sat there without reply.

'Bele Rina is a fool. Truth be told, she didn't say "no" to taking that old man's blood. Instead, she committed herself to giving all her own blood. Our venerable boss likes to say, "He who doesn't take blood gives blood."'

'Bele Rina is brave,' Karan wanted to interrupt him, but Acharya went on.

'This is not bravery on Bele Rina's part. It's sheer stupidity.'

Indicating that he was done with this conversation, Acharya rang the bell for the attendant.

'So Bacchu, is the theatre empty yet?'

'Yes, sir. Madam is free now.'

'Here, take your card, Mr Karan,' Acharya said. 'Mrs Woolworth can be a little gruff, but she will dispatch you quickly.'

'Namaste, babuji.'

Once they left Acharya's office, Bacchu proceeded to tease Karan. 'Bele Rina is gone.'

'Oh, I know.' Karan was no longer in the mood for conversation.

Mrs Woolworth actually did look angry. But when she poked the needle into Karan's arm and Karan's blood rapidly moved down the tube, filling the bottle, her pupils dilated and sparkled with joy, encircling him like vultures.

'Hee, hee, hee-hee!'

Seeing the blood flow uninterruptedly made her proud at her professional acumen, as if she were simply pouring blood from one bottle into another. And because she was beside herself with joy, she didn't feel even the slightest hesitation about what she was doing.

'Your body needs your own blood,' Bele Rina's whispers passed by Karan's ears and then disappeared the way they came.

He had already given a pint of blood, but Mrs Woolworth allowed the blood to continue flowing without asking Karan's permission.

Karan, too, kept staring at the tube without saying anything.

For a few more seconds, the blood continued to flow rapidly. But, once a pint and a half had been collected, the pace of the flow slackened till, eventually, only a few drops fell.

'That's enough.'

Coolly, Mrs Woolworth extracted the needle.

'Madam, shall I bring some coffee?'

'Yes,' bellowed Mrs Woolworth, as her eyebrows raised themselves out of habit, with her annoyance back firmly in place.

Karan slowly sipped his coffee and Mrs Woolworth filled out his chit and gave it to him. She then exited the theatre, leaving him alone.

'Sixty rupees!' Acharya exclaimed as he reviewed Karan's chit. 'You really are very lucky, Mr Karan. What more does a person with such rare blood need?'

'Work. I don't want money for my blood. I want work,' Karan replied.

'You will find that soon enough. Here, take this money for your blood and sign this receipt.'

On his way home, Karan stopped at a confectioner's shop.

'Give me half a seer of milk, very hot, and one of those pills for strength,' he said pointing at the board the confectioner had displayed.

'Yes, young man. Have a seat and relax. Observe the magic of Master Chanta.'

Chanta, the confectioner, kept twirling his professionally mandated moustache and smiled.

'The Mughal emperor heading to his harem would slip one of these pills into his mouth. My grandfather used to say . . .'

Karan adopted a look to make it seem as though he were listening to Chanta the confectioner very intently. He didn't know what he was thinking himself.

CHAPTER 5

Karan found a job—at three hundred rupees a month! Bebe had just returned from Ramjas's house. She was sitting in the courtyard cleaning rice to make khichdi. She always used that plate to clean the rice and lentils. When her daughter and son-in-law came to visit, she would seat them together and serve them in that same plate. When she was younger, she ate three square meals from that same plate, accompanied by her very hungry brother.

One did not eat openly with one's husband in those days. One could only do so in secret . . .

Bebe smiled and shook her head. She drew the now-soiled muslin dupatta that Karan had bought her over her head. If the plate were ever to be lost, several important links in Bebe's life would also be lost forever. Inside, in his room, Karan was filling out his job application, with the newspaper spread open in front of him.

'Mail!' the postman called from outside.

Bebe received the letter and brought it inside.

'Read this letter to me, son. It seems like it's from Labho.'

'I will be there as soon as I am done with this application. Wait for me in the courtyard.'

'I've told Labho so many times not to send letters. After all, you can write the same thing on a three-paisa postcard as in a six-paisa letter. What's the point in wasting three paisa?'

'Yes, Bebe. I will be right there as soon as I finish writing this application.'

There was an advertisement for a job at eighty rupees a month, with an eighteen-and-a-half-rupee inflation allowance. Karan's heart told him that he would definitely get this one. Two or three times, even as he wrote out the application, he stopped to get up and pray before the portrait of Guru Nanak. And Guru Nanak, too, seemed to affirm the notion that he would be successful this time. The heart of a dejected man is an empty vessel that he uses to give shape to his own feelings, so that sometimes when he feels hopeful for no reason, he will pick it up, despite its emptiness.

'Bebe, you'll see, I will definitely get this job. Guru Nanak Sahib agrees with me.'

He finished the application and went outside, to the courtyard.

'Now, son, read the letter to me.'

'What's this?' Karan exclaimed as he picked up the envelope. 'This letter is for me.'

He quickly opened the envelope and began reading the letter.

'Bebe! Be . . . Be!' Karan sat down in shock and happiness as he read the letter.

'I've gotten a job, Bebe! I have finally gotten a job! Three hundred rupees a month!'

Bebe's favourite plate slipped out of her hands, its contents scattering on the ground.

And the white grains of rice scattered all over the bare floor made it seem as if the entire courtyard were filled with grain!

'Really?!'

The plate made an impossible attempt to pull Bebe back towards its golden shine.

'Yes, Bebe, a full three hundred rupees a month!'

'Read the entire letter to me, son!'

Bebe kept looking at her hands that had become so dirty and rough from scrubbing Ramjas's pots with ash. She began to dream about how, from now on, she would spend all her days like Ramjas's sister-in-law, spinning yarn. She'd knit Karan a wonderful chequerboard-patterned shawl.

'Oh!' Bebe exclaimed when Karan had finished reading.

The hands that were rapidly spinning yarn, slowly, dejectedly, returned to washing pots.

'No, Bebe. It isn't for selling more blood. A friend of mine works there. His name is Acharya . . .'

'Acharya?'

Bebe momentarily forgot about Karan's job. 'Wait . . . I'd been reciting this auspicious name for several days. Do you remember the Pandit Maharaj who came last year? His name was also Acharyaji,' Bebe said, as she folded her palms and closed her eyes.

'I heard all of the verses of the Holy Gita from the sacred lips of that Pandit Maharaj.'

While Bebe, her eyes closed, was lost in thought about the Pandit Maharaj, Karan quickly reread the letter once more.

'Acharya has become my friend, Bebe. He's a very good man.'

'Yes, son. If there are no more good men, then the destruction of *kaliyug* would befall the world. The Pandit used to say . . .'

Bebe's attention now turned back towards her plate. She put it back upright and began picking grains of rice off the floor.

'The Pandit used to say . . .'

'Forget the Panditji, Bebe. Acharya says I need to go to the office tomorrow morning. The job has been finalized.'

Karan's blue eyes seemed like a stranger's as they embraced the arms of happiness and gratitude.

'This Acharya is such a good man. He never even mentioned the possibility of a job to me. He secretly worked to make things better.'

'Such men are hard to find, son. But I worry that the matter of giving blood will come up again.'

'No, Bebe. The job is somewhere else. Acharya says that he will introduce me to his boss. It's his boss who has arranged for this job.'

Bebe gathered all the grains of rice back into the plate. Their whiteness against the golden shine of the brass reminded her of a beautiful girl, all decked out, arriving at her wedding.

'Karne, my son. Now, all I want is to get you married. First, you need to get settled in your work, and then I will take care of all of the rest.'

'Don't worry about my wedding.'

It was as if Karan's own mother had come down from the heavens to observe her son's happiness and had hidden herself in the wrinkles on Bebe's forehead.

'Bebe, you should take better care of your health. I won't let you go to work at Ramjas's house any more. Let Ramjas's daughter-in-law go to hell. Three hundred rupees is no small sum, after all.'

'Yes, son. I was thinking the same thing. Once you are settled in your job, you just watch. I will pick a fight with Ramjas's daughter-in-law and come home. She is a very cruel woman.'

'You should consider my job all firmed up.'

Karan kept glancing at Acharya's letter.

'We simply can't understand God's plans, Bebe. Whatever he does, he does for the good.'

The goddess of happiness that was now in Karan's eyes gestured towards his faith, calling him closer.

'Last year, when I lost my job, I turned away from God as well. But man is not aware that whatever God does, he does in our best interests.'

Bebe, listening to his words, closed her eyes in piety, as if she was listening to Pandit Acharya Maharaj reciting the eighteenth chapter of the Bhagavad Gita.

'Son, about the things that you are saying, Pandit Maharaj said . . . What's his name again? Look, I've forgotten again . . . Well, it was just as meaningful as the things he was saying.'

'No, Bebe. Just think about it. If I hadn't lost my last job, my salary today would at most be one hundred and fifty rupees. But now I will get a full three hundred rupees.'

'Yes, how could we possibly think that the Almighty is a fool?' Bebe said, as she turned her attention back to the rice.

'Since this morning, my left eye has been twitching. My heart has been dejected all day.'

Bebe began separating the dirt and small stones from the rice. 'I hadn't thought about making khichdi in a long time. But today, I thought that I would feed my son khichdi dripping with ghee. Whether dejected or sad, the flute-playing Krishna provides the answer to each question in advance.'

Bebe occupied herself in preparing the khichdi. Karan got up and went into his room. There, he carelessly flung the job application that he had written off to the side and carefully placed his certificates away. He opened his trunk and took out the suit that he had gotten made with the earnings from his last job, but which he had only worn two or three times. The suit was wrinkled. He told himself that he would get it ironed from the laundry first thing in the morning.

He laid on the charpoy and began painting his future in beautiful colours. And his charpoy melded with the fantasy of those extravagant colours.

'Khaa . . . khoo . . . kho!'

Suddenly, out in the streets, Hakeem Sukh Chen's coughing seemed to be asking him something. Karan wished he would ask, 'So, Karan, found a job?'

'Namaste . . . Sir.'

Karan had been unable to forge a meaningful relationship with the Hakeem in so long that instead of addressing him as brother, uncle or friend—as he normally would have—he continued to address him formally.

'Namaste, Karanji?'

The Hakeem spoke in an inquisitive tone. He thought that Karan had perhaps come to his window, hearing him cough, because he wanted to ask him something.

'Are you alone? Are you in any pain?' Karan inquired, as he hoped that the Hakeem would ask him more about his job.

'I'm always in pain, brother.'

The Hakeem took out a packet of some medicine from the inside pocket of his coat. 'But what can one do?' he said, as he swallowed the contents of the packet.

'Khaa . . . khoo . . . kho . . . One has to handle one's responsibilities after all.'

'Have you received a letter from them?'

He was getting angry with the Hakeem for not asking about his job for the first time.

Calling Ragini 'them' almost stuck in his throat, and consequently, a strange noise emerged from his lips.

'From whom?'

'From Bhaa . . . bhi.'

He was still elated from the news of his job. And so, he did not feel any of his usual anguish associated with Ragini; he did miss her in her absence.

'Yes, brother. I have received many letters. Life becomes more difficult when a wife leaves home . . . Have you gotten any work?'

'Yes, sir . . . at three hundred rupees a month.'

The Hakeem looked at him in shock, because he didn't think that Karan was capable of jest.

'Yes, sir . . . Wait for a minute,' Karan said, as he leapt back and got Acharya's letter from the charpoy. 'Here, look at this.'

But the Hakeem didn't know English. Perhaps, this was the reason that he immediately believed Karan even without reading the letter.

'Three hundred rupees . . . That's very good, Karanji . . . I always used to tell Ragini that Karan has real potential, but she never agreed. Do not take offence; she is, after all, your sister-in-law. She used to say, he stands at his window the whole day, his mouth gaping, or he is lying down on his charpoy all day like a useless woman.'

As long as a man's heart and mind are drunk with laughter, he can find some explanation or another for the selfishness of friends and enemies. Perhaps for this reason, a person with a joyful disposition is usually non-violent and prone to forgiveness. So despite Ragini's comments about him, Karan's mind remained as calm as before.

'Bebe,' the Hakeem came up to the window and called out to Bebe. 'Bebe, are you inside?'

Bebe ran as fast as she could.

'Congratulations, Bebe. It's a very auspicious day.'

Then the Hakeem turned towards Karan and said in a patronizing tone, 'A mother is not only the one that gives birth; she can also be the one who steps in and takes over all the responsibilities of a mother!'

Bebe wiped the tears from her eyes with one hand while she caressed Karan's back with the other.

'My Karan is a very good boy, Hakeemji. Come, why are you standing outside? Won't you come inside? I've made khichdi today. You should have some as well.'

'Yes, Bebe. Who else is there to feed me these days? I will come in a short while.'

The Hakeem reached his door and stopped.

'O, chachi!' he called out as he saw two women from the neighbourhood. 'Have you heard? Bebe's Karan has gotten a job at three hundred rupees.'

'Really?'

Chachi looked over at her friend while subconsciously placing the fingers of her right hand on her chin. 'Really?'

Her companion's dupatta fell from her head, and her white hair caught the wind. She also seemed to be wondering, 'Really?'

'He's a very sweet and honest boy.'

'He doesn't even smoke cigarettes.'

'We should go and offer our congratulations to Bebe.'

Chachi grabbed her companion's arm and turned in the direction of Bebe's door, and, as if speaking privately, 'Arré, what is your opinion about Karan as a match for my Bhagwati?'

CHAPTER 6

The next day, Karan arrived fifteen minutes early for his appointment at the office of the People's Blood Bank.

Bacchu had just finished sweeping and cleaning Acharya's office and was sitting on a stool outside.

'Namaste, babuji.'

Bacchu admired the charming new suit on Karan's fair, slim body and, awestruck, stood up immediately. And perhaps he began to think about Bele Rina.

'Namaste!'

Oddly, Karan now seemed to be very aware of his good looks and his stylish get-up. When the hope of riches knocks on the door of a poor man's hut, instead of running to greet it, he preoccupies himself with his own appearance. And he remains lost for so long that the hope of luxury too is left waiting interminably—so much so that that it turns into the expectation of exhaustion.

'So, has Acharya Sahib arrived?'

Karan's honour, fallen and humiliated for so long, tried to lift itself up again, and this gave his voice a ridiculous tone.

'No, he hasn't arrived yet, babuji.'

Bacchu brought him into Acharya's office very respectfully, as if he had come to buy back his own blood from the People's Blood Bank.

'Babuji, if Madam had been here today, she would have been very pleased to see you dressed up like this.'

'Madam, who?'

Sitting on the chair, Karan took a handkerchief from his pocket and dusted the pleats of his pants and his shoes.

'Madam Bele Rina.'

Still dusting, he was a little taken aback by Bacchu's observation. 'Why did he think of Bele Rina when he saw me?'

'And tell me, just what reason would she have for being happy?' he asked.

'She was in love with you.'

Bacchu said it with the same conviction that he had when he had seen the two of them drinking brandy together in the theatre.

'Love . . . !'

The impoverished innocence around Karan's face transformed it into a smile—a pendulum arc, like dolls on a swing. For a moment, he forgot about his current get-up. And when people are less conscious of their own beauty, they appear even more beautiful.

'Babuji, that day after you left, Madam was very sad. She drank a lot of brandy in an attempt to forget her sorrow. In the evenings, I was the one who dropped her off at her home.'

'Home . . . ?! Where is her home?'

All Karan wanted was to get up and set out for Bele Rina's house, but he remained seated.

'She doesn't live there any more. I don't know where she is now. One day I went to check on her, but she wasn't there.'

His hopes, once hot like a wood fire, were now doused with water from an upturned pail.

'Wasn't there?'

'No!'

In front of them was the picture of a man, smiling peacefully as his blood was being drawn. The picture was upturned though and was now hanging upside down in the room. Bacchu went on to straighten it out.

'Madam was a very good woman.'

'Yes!'

The hissing sounds of the wood fire being extinguished were now deafening.

'When I went to drop her off at her home, babuji, she said a lot of things to me.'

'What kinds of things did she say?'

Karan was as eager as a child waiting to hear his favourite fairy tale. His entire body, a giant ear.

'She talked of how handsome you were. That is why I believe that she loved you tremendously. She would

often wonder why such ethereal beauty was so close
by? Now, how could I respond? She answered her own
question, "God's beauty is so close by because the rich
embody the true ugliness of man." Babuji, now isn't that
a deep thought!'

'Yes.'

'Then, in her drunkenness, she burst into tears. I was
scared so I got a taxi. Once we were in the taxi, she told
me her whole story of grief.'

'Don't stop. Please continue,' Karan prompted
impatiently when Bacchu went momentarily quiet.

'Madam's family is very poor,' Bacchu resumed.

'Her brother sold his wife's honour over and over,
and lived off of it. Once he even sold Madam's honour.
What else could the poor man do, babuji? You came here
to sell your blood twice. You didn't do it of your own free
will. Madam's brother, too, must have agonized over
trading his wife's and sister's honour.'

'Yes.'

Karan had become so engrossed in listening to
Bele Rina's story that he didn't even register his own
responses.

'Over time, Madam became sick and tired of selling
her honour, and so she took a course in nursing. She
wanted to serve people by becoming a nurse, but she
had to take a job with our company. She hated the work
that the company did, babuji. When she was talking to
me, she kept cursing all the men at the company in
English. She cursed herself as well . . . and . . . and . . .

and she grabbed both of my hands and said . . . You are my brother, my father, you are poor, and you should sell my honour, too . . .!'

Overwhelmed, Bacchu was completely out of breath.

'There is definitely one benefit to alcohol, babuji. Once drunk, a man stops caring about his joys and sorrows and, like a naked infant, achieves a pure and loving joy about the world.'

Just then, Mrs Woolworth barged into the office to sign the attendance register.

'Good morning.'

'Good morning, Mrs Woolworth!'

Karan got up from his chair, and he noticed that the usually dry and morose face looked pleasantly filled with cool and blessed rain clouds.

'Good morning, madam.'

The unusually happy expression on Mrs Woolworth's face made Bacchu so shocked and nervous that he overturned a bottle of ink on Acharya's table.

'Oh . . . you?' Mrs Woolworth removed her glasses and began to size up Karan.

'Have you come to give blood again today?'

'No!'

Karan was jolted back to the actual reason of his presence in the office. Suddenly, he felt agitated over the fact that Acharya still hadn't arrived at the office.

'Does Mr Acharya always come in late?' he asked Bacchu, who was still staring at Mrs Woolworth in wonderment.

'You seem very happy today.'

In truth, Mrs Woolworth was seeing a reflection of her own happiness in Karan's face.

'I like the colour of your suit very, very much. My son, Jimmy, also likes green very much.'

'So, are you very happy today, madam?' Bacchu couldn't help but ask as he cleaned the spilt ink from Acharya's table.

'Yes, I am very happy today. I got a letter today from my son, Jimmy, from Africa. He's found a job!'

'Your son is in Africa?' Karan asked.

'Yes, he couldn't find any kind of work here. His uncle asked him to join him in Africa. But even there, he had been unable to find any work for two years, until now.'

Karan said to himself, 'This is not the woman who took my blood last time. That woman's face was stretched tight, like a blister. But this woman is a mother separated from her child, and today, she is beside herself at the news of her son's gainful employment. The painful pus inside of the blister has vanished.'

'Do you plan to join your son there, madam?'

Bacchu watched as Mrs Woolworth laughed out loud, apparently lost in a joyful dream.

'Yes, when my Jimmy calls me over, I will definitely go. Jimmy's father has been paralysed for the last two years. He can't even get up from bed. But this news has worked a miracle. Out of sheer happiness, he got up and began to walk, and that, too, without the doctor's medicine!'

The dark rain clouds in the sky were beginning to drizzle.

'You look just like my Jimmy in this green suit,' she said, addressing Karan.

'Come here and kiss Mummy on her temple like Jimmy used to do.'

Karan hesitated. But the force of the imploring look of maternal affection made him concede. He bent down to kiss a smiling lock of white hair near Mrs Woolworth's temple.

'Thank you.'

Not losing her smile for even an instant, Mrs Woolworth marked her presence in the attendance register placed in a corner of the room.

'Okay, babuji, I will sit outside. Acharyaji should be here any moment now.'

'Why hasn't he arrived yet?' Karan, worried once again, wanted to ask Bacchu.

But Bacchu had already turned around to leave.

'Namaste, babuji!'

As he reached the door, Bacchu greeted the stenographer, Mrs Chaddha, 'Namaste, sister!'

Mrs Chaddha responded by throwing an irritated look at him. She had repeatedly admonished Bacchu to address her as 'madam' instead of 'sister'.

'Idiot . . .!' she mumbled curses at Bacchu out of his earshot.

'Good morning, Mrs Chaddha.'

The uncharacteristic warmth in Mrs Woolworth's voice startled Mrs Chaddha.

'Good morning, Mrs Woolworth!'

Once Mrs Chaddha had also marked her presence, both the ladies left together.

'Mrs Chaddha, my son Jimmy has . . . Hello! Good morning, Mr Acharya . . .'

It was as if Mrs Woolworth had lost control and began laughing wildly.

As he entered the room, Acharya observed Mrs Woolworth's uncharacteristic happiness and forgot to respond to her greetings.

Once the two women left, Acharya turned his attention to Karan.

'Namaste, Mr Karan. You've arrived.'

'Namaste, Acharyaji.'

Karan got up from his seat, overcome with feelings of gratitude.

'Please, have a seat.'

Acharya also marked his presence in the register and sat in his own chair.

'My bus was delayed today.'

He began to light a cigarette.

'What is the matter with Mrs Woolworth today? This is the first time . . .'

'Her son has gotten a job in Africa.'

'Oh . . . that explains it.'

Acharya offered Karan a cigarette. He wanted to say no but for the sake of Acharya's kind gesture, he accepted.

'You also seem to be in very good spirits today. And why not, arrangements for your job have also been finalized.'

'Acharyaji, I . . . I am eternally grateful to you.'

'It's fine. But really, you should be grateful to my boss. He was the one who needed the services of a young man for some friend of his. I suggested your name, and things worked out for you.'

'If you hadn't helped me out, I don't know where I would be. With all my heart, I am grateful to you, Acharyaji.

'Okay, stop with all of this gratitude nonsense now . . . I am completely overwhelmed by how you've made yourself up today. That woman . . . what was her name . . . Bele Rina, if she had caught even a glimpse of you today, she would have ground the flour for your rotis for the rest of your life.'

Acharya opened a few files in front of him, giving Karan an impression that he was pretty occupied with work.

'Who knows what kind of social service she is wasting her life on now.'

One of the files took on the appearance of Bele Rina's profile in Acharya's eyes, and began to breathe.

'Say what you will, but she was a very kind-hearted woman . . .'

He turned away from Bele Rina's profile to stare at Karan . . .

'Can I tell you something, Mr Karan?'

'Please do.'

Karan was anticipating a conversation about the details of the job. In his excitement, he took a very long drag from his cigarette, and immediately began to cough . . .

Acharya's frank disposition could not suppress a smile.

'What I cannot fathom is why you even need to work. If you were smart about it you would realize that all of the women of the world would work twenty-four hours a day for you. God has given you such a beautiful face . . . Why are you nervous? Why are you in such a rush to get to work?'

Suddenly, Ragini was beating out a rhythm and unloading lullabies in Karan's ears.

Karan sat up straight like a child who had just been shaken.

'Are you trying to say, Acharyaji, that women should toss me around in their hands like a toy? Those sort of toys are easily broken and smashed.'

'All beautiful people have the same misconception. The poor wretches can't even understand a simple, straightforward matter. Their beauty always seems to blind their intelligence. Listen, brother, grab a hold of your intelligence as you go forward. Why do you have to become a toy? . . . And truth be told, women don't even like toys . . . They want mischievous butter thieves, like Krishna, the kind who would leave them in tears one day, laughing and smiling, returning permanently to

Vrindavan. Dear brother, why don't you heed the wisdom of the Gita? Put in a little effort, then watch as these flirtatious women turn into your playthings and dance at a mere glance from you.'

The middle-aged Acharya kept talking about Krishna's antics a little white longer. But when his cigarette went out, he paused the monologue to light it again.

'I spent all of last night reading about the life of Krishna. Well, what else can an old person like me read?'

'Acharyaji, my job . . .?'

'Oh right, I had all but forgotten about that. This is my one weakness. Once an interesting topic comes up, I forget the immediate issue at hand.'

In the meantime, a young man, a clerk, entered the room to mark himself present in the attendance register.

'Arshad, late again today?'

'The bus was late, Acharyaji.'

'Your bus shouldn't be late. Understand?!'

Once Arshad had left, Acharya began speaking to Karan again.

'The successful man never lets an opportunity slip through his fingers. Mr Karan, the unsuccessful types are always the ones whose bus is late . . . Once an opportunity is gone, one cannot acquire anything else except regret.'

As Karan's eyes widened, he inquired, 'Why are you explaining all of this to me?'

'I am telling you all of this because your job is of a rather strange variety. But for you, this is a golden opportunity. You should not miss this chance. Come, let me take you to my boss.'

'But can you first provide me with some details?'

The Acharya's mysterious tone made Karan afraid that his job might involve something illegal. He had read in novels that rich men often took advantage of the desperation of the poor and young, and made them the prey of their various illegal operations.

'Don't be afraid. Your job is definitely unusual but it is very safe work. The Sardar Bahadur will give you the details himself.'

Acharya put out his cigarette and stood up. 'My boss's name is Sardar Bahadur Dr Shamsher Singh, but he doesn't wear a beard. He often produces formal letters. Come, let's go.'

Both of them left the room and went through the corridor. Acharya came to a brisk halt in front of a large door and knocked gently.

'Come in!'

Stepping inside with Acharya into this solemn space gave Karan the impression that he had just entered a marvellous shrine.

'Sir, this is Mr Karan. The one to whom we sent the employment letter.'

'Good morning, sir!'

'Oh . . . Yes! Good morning, Mr Karan.' The quivering organ inside those fat lips looked like a snake's flickering tongue. Two beady eyes stared at Karan's face, blinking rapidly. The bald head nodded in assent.

'Have a seat. Let me first have a look at this circular from the Ministry of Health.'

Karan sat down, quietly examining the room he was in.

There were thick, red velvet drapes hanging over the windows with some gap letting very little light in. And, in the soft darkness of the room, a red light bulb shone like a god's jewel that the owner of the People's Blood Bank had somehow acquired.

On the tiles of the floor, an expensive carpet, also red, had been laid out, and in the light of the bulb, it looked like it had been drenched with blood. Behind the boss, and above him, was a very large wall painting. Soon Karan was ignoring everything else, his entire attention fixed on the painting.

Suddenly Karan felt Acharya's foot pressing on his own under the table, in at attempt to get his attention back to the task at hand.

'Acharya . . .!'

'Yes, sir . . .!'

'Give this circular to the nurse and this draft to the typist . . . Go!'

The bald head, bent over in work, now lifted up, and the snake's tongue, as if looking for milk, flickered even more rapidly.

Watching the 'Sardar Bahadur' sent a shiver down Karan's spine. A shiver that spelt an unnameable fear.

'If there is any pending work remaining, Mr Karan, I get uneasy. Mr Acharya, why are you still standing here?'

'Sir, Mr Karan . . .'

'I will talk to Mr Karan myself,' Sardar Shamsher Singh said to him imperiously. 'You should go . . .'

Now, Karan was certain that this was an attempt to trap him in some dubious scheme. What if it were a robbery or a plan to loot someone. 'These days, when you can find hundreds of people to do any work for a meagre monthly income, why have I been offered three hundred rupees?' he wondered.

'Mr Karan!'

'Yes, sir!' Karan's response sounded inexplicably higher and cracked.

'Don't be nervous.'

The Sardar Bahadur's beady eyes blinked repeatedly as they sized up Karan's person.

'I am happy that you are healthy and that you are so well dressed. That is basically why you have been found to be qualified for this proposed work.'

Karan's innocent blue eyes impatiently and nervously queried, 'What is the proposed work?'

'How far have you studied?'

'BA, honours, in English.'

'Very good! On account of your personality and your education you are perfectly suited for this work.'

'But what will I be doing?'

And then suddenly conscious of his tone, Karan rephrased his question to sound more professional.

'What I mean is, sir, I am still unaware of the nature of my job.'

'That is the reason you have been summoned here.'

It felt as if Sardar Bahadur Dr Shamsher Singh were taking pleasure in Karan's confusion.

'You must have heard of Dr Bakhtiyar, yes?'

'No, sir.'

'That's surprising. Well, he is a famous retired doctor from our city and is the inventor of several important medicines. He is in need of a personal secretary immediately. The salary is three hundred rupees a month.'

Seeing Karan breathe a sigh of relief, the boss of the People's Blood Bank gave out a light smile.

'Do you accept?'

'Yes, sir! Thank you very much, sir!'

Karan wanted to say a lot more to express his gratitude and willingness to work, but he could not find the right words.

'But . . .' added the boss.

Karan, till this moment a happy, smiling child, was once again overcome with worry that something would crash into his newly constructed home of possibilities.

'But, there will be one more responsibility in your job.'

'I will make every effort to honour all of my responsibilities happily.'

The Sardar Bahadur gestured to him to remain silent.

'Dr Bakhtiyar has become very old and quite weak, and your blood type matches his blood type.'

Karan's heart skipped a beat.

'But there is no reason to be afraid. He won't have much need for your blood very often. Dr Bakhtiyar has a serious health complex and his, as well as your, blood type is very rare. This is why he is looking for a young man to be his secretary, who can also give his own blood exactly when he needs it. He is going to have a major operation after some time, and at that time his need for blood will likely increase. Tell me, do you accept?'

Karan's face fell and his head hung down, his eyes staring at the floor.

'Be . . . Be. I've got a job!'

'Don't fall into this blood nonsense again.'

'Three hundred rupees, Bebe! Three hundred rupees is no small sum!'

'You accept this post, don't you, Mr Karan?'

Like a dumb beast surrounded, Karan didn't know what he said as he struck a pose to say yes.

'Very good! I will write you a letter of introduction. Go to Dr Bakhtiyar's place tomorrow with the letter.'

While the boss of the People's Blood Bank wrote the letter of introduction, Karan lifted his head to stare, once again, at the wall painting behind him.

In the painting, nature was sleeping in its twilight, and in her lap, a dam of dense, strong human blood shone brightly. Deep into the image, a redness filled the shades of the thick trees, and in the background of this deep red shade, yellow romantic creatures spread out like fog. These vaporous bodies took solace from their enfeeblement as they slowly advanced towards the lake of blood.

'Are you wondering about the painting?' Sardar Bahadur Dr Shamsher Singh stopped in the middle of writing the letter.

'It's an excellent painting.'

He lowered his bald head back into the letter.

Karan couldn't bear the sense of pain he experienced on behalf of the lifeless creatures.

'Who are these people?'

'The sick!'

'And this lake of blood?'

'We have collected the surplus blood of humanity here. Because of these reserves of blood, the trapped sick can heal.'

A number of thoughts came rushing into Karan's mind. He wanted to respond with, 'No, the surplus blood of humanity is not collected here. This blood has been squeezed from the dry bones of the poor. It is the well-to-do who have surplus blood in their healthy bodies, blood whose headiness courses through them, overwhelming and intoxicating them.

'And these sick creatures are really us. We have filled this damned lake with the blood that we have sold over and over again, and still we stumble and fall in these red shadows, inching our way towards the dam, so that we can dump our remaining blood into this reservoir.

'And this stockpile of our blood allows the brokers to collect stacks of cash in their vaults, stacks so big that like simple folk, they forget even to count them.'

But Karan's thoughts and ideals, arising from his poverty, didn't even have enough cloth to clothe their bodies. If they were to stand naked, face-to-face with the owner of the People's Blood Bank, they would have become the object of derision, and so Karan remained silent.

'Here, take the letter.'

This was the instant when Karan abandoned his freedom and got up from his chair.

'I've written Dr Bakhtiyar's address on the outside of the envelope.'

'Thank you, sir.'

When he left Sardar Bahadur Dr Shamsher Singh's room, Karan was filled with a deep ensemble of agony. The fate of Marlowe's Doctor Faustus danced before his eyes—Faustus, who had sold his soul to the devil in exchange for strength, wealth and pleasure.

Karan's thoughts became increasingly bitter. 'In the beginning, Satan paid large sums merely to purchase souls. But in our times, human blood can be acquired for pennies. And, if blood could be bought and sold, then the soul would comply of its own accord. And now that Satan could see this, why would he waste his energy and money chasing after souls?'

'So, Mr Karan, what are you thinking about?'

He ran into Acharya in the corridor.

'Did you get the job?'

'Yes!' he responded, his voice filled with exhaustion.

'Then, friend, you should be happy. Why do you sound so defeated?'

'Acharya . . .' Karan's present emotional state prevented him from acknowledging Acharya's seniority. 'I've basically declared war on my conscience by accepting the job you arranged.'

Acharya slapped Karan on the back and said, 'Forget about your conscience. Just take care of your health. Should Dr Bakhtiyar want one pint of blood, be sure to give him four pints, and that too by eating his food and staying at his place. Do you understand?'

He shook Karan's hand with great excitement.

'Best of luck.'

In response, Karan let out an anaemic laugh.

'Come, I'll walk you out.'

'Thank you.'

Karan's aloofness made Acharya very uncomfortable. He felt like he should comfort the young man. 'If you do your work cleverly, it's possible that you wouldn't have to give him blood very regularly.'

CHAPTER 7

Dayal Bagh Road had been driven mad by the noise of one of the city's central squares, and so covering its ears, it took off to the left. A mile and a half or two miles on, it still didn't look back. Once it reached the ironsmith's well, it stopped for a while to rest, and then proceeded slowly on to a desolate neighbourhood, ending at the graveyard.

'So, sister, what news have you brought?'

All of the residents of the graveyard became restless to get out.

'What is the price of milk these days? My darling child will get his milk, right?'

'Has my Afzal found a job?'

'Hah . . . hai! The pain in my shoulders! It took my life, but it still pursues me. So, sister, is a doctor's treatment still expensive?'

'My darling child will get his milk, right?'

'I've just come back from peeking through the torn curtain of our door. *Didi?* Who looks after my elderly mother and father now?'

'My darling child will . . .'

'Oh . . . Shut up!'

From a marble grave, a loud, awe-inspiring voice boomed. The tiny tombs in the damp, raw earth put fingers across their lips.

'Looking over at those tombs always makes me feel like the corpses are secretly talking to one another.'

Dr Bakhtiyar and his daughter were headed home after their evening stroll. Their home had always stood lonely, right at the back of the graveyard.

'This is exactly why the things you say scare me, Papa.' Ms Bakhtiyar swept her short hair back, and began walking faster. 'Your thinking is very strange.'

'Walk more slowly, Baby. Walking this quickly taxes my lungs.'

'Papa, I am scared of this haunted area! Are such places even meant for living and breathing humans?'

'What is it to you? I am the one who is going to have to stay here . . . Walk even more slowly.' Dr Bakhtiyar stopped to catch his breath.

'You only come to visit occasionally, during your college holidays. And soon, you will be leaving for England in a month or two, and then even those visits won't happen.'

'No, Papa. The image of this house will terrify me in England as well . . .'

She stopped mid-sentence, perhaps losing herself in her beautiful thoughts, imagining herself in some English dance hall in the arms of a strange white youth, feeling herself tremble.

'Papa, you've sent in the application form for my passport, haven't you?'

'Yes!'

Dr Bakhtiyar continued, 'Baby, initially, I, too, was afraid of the images of tombs. But when we moved here, I felt as if I belonged here . . . Your mother used to say the say the same thing. She was the one who proposed the name for this house, Aaraam Gah [the rest house or the graveyard].'

'Aaraam Gah . . . This graveyard . . . A rest house? . . . It's when you talk like this that my heart sinks. Come, let's go quickly.'

'Zahra, let's visit your mother's grave on our way.'

'No, Papa. I want to go home now.'

'Okay, whatever you want.'

Dr Bakhtiyar made a futile attempt to laugh and then lit his cigar.

'Do you never think about your mother, Zahra? It often seems to me that she gets out of her grave and comes to Aaraam Gah, and she wanders around from room to room like she used to do when she was alive. When she was alive, Zahra, she used to tell me all the time to stop smoking cigars. I still feel like she is here, snatching the cigars from my fingers.'

'Don't say such things, Papa. I . . . I . . .'

'You feel frightened, don't you? I fear all this talk of death, too, Zahra, but my illness has made me accustomed to this fear. That's why it doesn't terrify me any more. I . . . Oh, why has your face turned so sallow? Even though you are an educated . . .'

'No, Papa. It's not that.'

Zahra was attempting to appear brave.

'I am only afraid of the things you say.'

'But I am speaking about your mother, my daughter. This house is mine, hers and yours. Even after death, she has full control over her house.'

'Nonsense.'

Zahra had really forgotten her fear and passionately presented her argument.

'After death, our existence is completely wiped out. These are all matters for the living. We are nothing after death. All traces of us are completely erased.'

'That's why I am afraid of death. I want to live on like this even after I die.'

Dr Bakhtiyar placed his hand on the left side of his chest.

'Look, my heart is racing. The slightest bit of excitement becomes completely unbearable.'

'Papa, let's not talk about this any more. As soon as we get home, go straight to your room, close the door and lie down quietly.'

'Quietly? . . . No, Baby! I don't like lying down quietly at all . . . I am still alive . . . Even after I die, I won't lie down quietly in my grave . . . You wouldn't understand, but even after death, our existence isn't wiped out entirely. It remains intact, just as before. I am certain that every morning, I will get up from my grave and come to Aaraam Gah . . . To shave!'

Zahra felt a shiver run through her, but she also felt pity for her father.

'Poor Papa! Why do you even think about death? After the operation, you will be completely fine.'

Like a child, Dr Bakhtiyar snuggled up very close to his daughter, as if he had caught the scent of compassion and wanted to turn over his feelings of helplessness to his daughter.

'Help me walk, Baby.'

Zahra wrapped her left arm around his waist.

'Baby, I've created more than twenty medicines, but you are my best creation. I find such joy in having you close to me.'

'Oh . . . Poor Papa!'

Zahra lovingly tightened her grip on the old man's waist.

'A little gently, Baby.'

Zahra loosened her hold as he said, 'Will you do one thing for me?'

'What?'

'Stay here until I have my operation. What's the rush with your education? It will still be there in another year!'

'What do you mean?'

'What I mean is, you can leave for England next year. Stay here until I have my operation.'

'Oh . . . no! No, Papa!'

Zahra removed her arm from around Dr Bakhtiyar's waist.

'But all of the arrangements for my admission have already been taken care of. How can I possibly do what you are asking?'

The old man observed her state of beautiful exasperation, which reminded him of an elderly poet's youthful memory, in whose image he would forget how old he had become. He felt almost as if his late wife stood before him, looking like a maiden now. She also used to become distressed exactly like this, and Dr Bakhtiyar would placate her with love and kindness.

Seeing Dr Bakhtiyar go silent, his eyelids drooping from the weight of the past, Zahra softened.

'Okay, if this is what you really want, I won't go.'

'No, you were right, Baby. It will mean wasting an entire year unnecessarily.'

Zahra breathed a sigh of relief.

After the pretence of agreeing to a sacrifice but then being immediately released from that obligation, a human's moral sensibility becomes like a soldier who emerged victorious without a single scratch, puffing out its chest with pride.

Dr Bakhtiyar had hoped that Zahra would accede to staying with him until the operation, but, seeing her silence, he pursed his lips in angry disappointment.

'Papa,' Zahra wrapped her left arm around his waist again, 'when is the man from the blood bank coming over?'

The old man quickly became subdued.

'On the phone Dr Shamsher Singh said that he would be here by 9 o'clock tomorrow morning.'

'I will explain every detail of your care to him with extreme care. You are going to be perfectly fine, Papa.'

They arrived at the door to Aaraam Gah's enormous structure.

'Smile, Papa. Please smile!'

Dr Bakhtiyar removed the cigar from his lips and smiled at his daughter.

'Oh!' He returned the cigar to his lips. 'The pain has returned under my left kidney.'

'You should go to your room and lie down,' Zahra said in an exhausted, annoyed voice. 'I will tell the servant to bring you a hot-water bottle.'

Once her father had left, she called out for the servant.

'Coming, Babyji.'

From one of the rooms nearby, the pudgy, short Bobby tumbled like a ball only to stop at her feet.

'Take a hot-water bottle upstairs to the master.'

'Yes, Babyji.'

Bouncing, the ball quickly tumbled out of sight.

Zahra looked at her watch and exclaimed, 'Oh, it's time for BBC Music, and I didn't even notice . . .'

She headed towards the drawing room.

'I always miss my favourite songs when Papa starts with his absurd talk.'

CHAPTER 8

There is a certain sense of familiarity to beautiful faces—a singular sharpness, a distinctive expression, a natural grace. This is why, even when we meet an attractive person for the first time, we feel as though we have known them, deeply.

'Oh . . . You?'

As Zahra came into the drawing room where Karan was already seated, she looked over at him and felt a distinct past connection with the grave, rakish face.

'Ji, my name is M.A. Karan.'

Karan got up from the sofa as soon as he saw her.

'Please. Don't get up.'

Brooding, attractive faces held a very appealing quality for Zahra, like cold orange ice cream.

'Please, have a seat.'

His charming face and its infinite sadness reminded her of Akhtar's face. Akhtar, with whom she had flirted for the first time several years ago.

Even while sitting, Karan's posture was so stiff and straight, it gave the impression that he was still standing.

'So tell me . . .!'

Zahra's heart was shrouded in the newly awakened dense shadows of memories of her first romance. She sat down on the sofa next to Karan.

'I've been sent by the People's Blood Bank, for the job . . .'

'Very good!'

She took Shamsher Singh's letter from him and then went on to survey him with a brazen look like Cleopatra's, a look filled with entitlement.

'This letter is for the Doctor Sahib.'

'I am Dr Bakhtiyar's daughter.'

She responded as she opened the envelope, as if to say, 'The Doctor Sahib is my child. He does nothing without my consent.'

'Are you married, Mr Karan?' she curtly asked Karan as she finished reading the letter.

'No,' said Karan, looking at her, puzzled.

'Or, a girlfriend?'

'Girlfriend?'

Karan became anxious.

'Ji, no!'

'Fine.'

Zahra bestowed him with a sweet smile.

'Do you have any hobbies?'

'Hobbies?'

Karan could not figure out how to respond.

'Do we have a guest, Baby?'

In the meantime, Dr Bakhtiyar had entered the room.

'This is Mr Karan M.A., Daddy.'

Karan wanted to correct her.

'I mean, M.A. Karan. He's been sent by the People's Blood Bank.'

'Good morning, sir!'

Dr Bakhtiyar sat down.

'Please sit down.'

'The Sardar Bahadur has sent over this letter, Daddy.'

Dr Bakhtiyar read the letter.

'Well, Mr Karan.' Zahra turned back towards Karan.

'What are your hobbies? For instance, Music . . . Cinema . . . Dancing . . .?'

'Why are you asking such irrelevant questions, Baby?' Dr Bakhtiyar said, now, folding up the letter. 'Cinema, dancing . . . Mr Karan hasn't been called here to rehearse scenes.'

Zahra looked at Karan as if to say, 'That's exactly why you've been summoned here, right?'

'So, you have a BA with honours?' Dr Bakhtiyar asked. 'And Shamsher Singh has explained to you all of the requirements of this job?'

'Yes, sir.' Karan sounded dejected, like a person who had resigned himself to his merciless fate.

'I have a severe shortage of blood, and I have need for a pint or two of blood regularly. Except sometimes a little more frequently. I have been scheduled for an operation on my gall bladder shortly. I will need extra blood at that time.'

'Let's talk about something else, Daddy.' Zahra wanted to talk to Karan about herself. 'Mr Karan has said that all of these points have already been explained to him.'

'Just wait a moment, Baby. Let us finish talking about work-related matters first.'

Dr Bakhtiyar turned to face Karan again.

'The real work is actually about the blood, Mr Karan. The job of the secretary is very easy, although that is important as well. My health no longer permits me to pay the deserved attention to my patented medicine business. A few companies are selling my medicines in the market. From now on, you will manage all the correspondence with them. All that remains are a few of my personal affairs, and Zahra will explain those to you.'

'Yes, Papa, I will explain everything,' Zahra said, annoyed.

'And your salary will be three hundred rupees. All right?'

'Yes, sir!'

'Oh, yes, one more thing . . . It's essential that you live here in order to take proper care of me. The guest quarters are on the top floor.'

'Thank you, sir.'

'You should take your meals with us here. All right?'

Just then, Zahra's pet Alsatian waddled into the room and sat down next to his mistress. He wagged his tail in excitement, making a show of his restlessness.

Zahra wrapped her arms around the dog's healthy waist and brought its face up to her cheek.

'My sweet dog!'

'Yes, sir!' Karan replied to Dr Bakhtiyar. He was already scheduling his visits to Bebe a few times each week.

Struggling to get back up on his feet, Dr Bakhtiyar said, 'I will be in my office. Tell Bobby that I will take my medicine there . . . Uff!'

'All right, Papa!'

Zahra let go of the dog's waist, so he stood up on his hind legs and began to climb up on his mistress.

'Hey! Naughty boy!' Zahra smiled at Karan. It wasn't clear if she was addressing Karan or the dog.

'I feel a sharp pain under my right kidney,' Dr Bakhtiyar said, pausing at the door. 'Tell Bobby to bring my medicine to my bedroom and a hot-water bottle, too.'

He left the room very slowly.

'Excuse me!' Zahra turned to address Karan. 'I will be right back.'

'Bob—by!'

Karan heard another voice replying, 'I am coming, madam!'

The floor echoed with the sound of a bouncing ball.

'Bobby, go and give Papa his medicine in his bedroom upstairs. And take a hot-water bottle, too.'

'Yes, Babyji.'

Having dismissed the servant, Zahra returned to Karan.

'Poor Papa! I feel really sorry for him, Mr Karan.'

Zahra's darling dog had left the room. And in his place, she imagined Karan standing close to her, by her side, wagging his tail wildly, so that she could put her hands around his waist and nuzzle her face against his neck.

'Poor, poor Papa!'

'Yes, the poor man's illness troubles him terribly.'

'Troubles? No, Mr Karan.'

Zahra turned philosophical. She turned around to call out for her dog: 'Toto! Toto!'

Toto ran in, raised his front legs and placed them on Zahra's shoulders.

'No, Mr Karan. Not just troubles. If that were the case, the human soul would not remain so unsettled.'

In truth, she was thinking less about her father and more about finding ways to keep talking to him, to find the appropriate words to make Karan understand that he should fall for her quickly, because he was going to fall for her inevitably.

'I am very sorry, Ms . . . Ms Bakhtiyar.'

Zahra stood up in amazement.

'Come! I will show you around Aaraam Gah.'

'Let's go.'

'Perhaps, now that you've arrived, my boredom will dissipate. Ever since I left the university hostel, this Aaraam Gah feels like hell to me.'

'You were boarding in the university hostel?'

And as he said that, Karan thought to himself, 'Or what else? That's what she was telling you.'

'Yes. It's only been two months since I received my MA and came back here.'

'Splendid!'

Karan was trying to sound relaxed and calm.

'What subject did you get your MA in?'

'English literature!'

They left the room and walked down the beautiful corridor outside together.

'Are you also interested in literature, Mr Karan?'

'Yes, of course! I graduated with honours in English literature as well.'

'Lovely! As for me, I don't care if I eat or not, but I must have new books.'

Karan wanted to explain to her, 'Madam, the hungry are just as deceived by books as they are by the promise of bread. Perhaps, that is why the poor wretches are fated neither for bread nor for education.'

But instead he said, 'Your hobby is worthy of admiration.'

'I often wonder why people consider *Lady Chatterley's Lover* obscene? I have enjoyed the book thoroughly. Have you read it?'

'No.'

'I will give it to you tomorrow. You're coming tomorrow morning, right?'

'Yes.'

'Fine. Here we are. This is Papa's office. Papa has discovered some of the best medicines to help people, but now he is very distressed about his own poor health. Poor dear Papa! Papa's library is in that room. It's been locked for some time now. It's mostly medical books, otherwise I would have been in there all the time. Are you interested in medical books, Mr Karan?'

'No, Ms . . . Ms Bakhtiyar.'

'Me, neither. Those books use very convoluted language. But to help Papa in his work, you will need to familiarize yourself with a few medical terms. I will have the library opened up for you to refer to. At the end of this corridor is our garage. Uncle Fazlu's garage. Uncle Fazlu is our driver, but he runs his tongue far more than he does the car . . .'

Karan smiled and turned in that direction.

'To the left of the garage is the garden that you came through. The white roses in our garden bloom all year round. Did you notice the white roses, Mr Karan?'

'Sorry, Ms Bakhtiyar. I was absorbed in my thoughts.'

'I noticed that, that you are often lost in thought.'

There was a subtle change in Zahra's tone now, the notes of a smile slipping into her voice.

'The colour of our white roses matches your complexion. I always use the white-rose shade of powder. At the top of the staircase is a full suite. That's the one that you would be staying in. The room next to it, the middle room, is my bedroom. The stairs in front of the drawing room lead to Papa and Mummy's master suite.

My mother was very sweet, Mr Karan. She could have easily passed for my older sister even in her last days. She passed away last year. Poor, dear Mummy!'

'I am very sorry, indeed!'

'Come, let me show you to your room.' They ascended the stairs together.

'Mr Karan, during the time that my mother died, I was in my college hostel in Bombay. That evening, I had gone to Jolly Sailor's dance club with my friends. When the telegram arrived at my hostel, the superintendent sent it forward to the club. When I received the news there, I fell unconscious right into Jolly Sailor's arms. Poor, dear mother—!'

Zahra paused, fingering the handkerchief in her pocket.

'I am really sorry, Ms Bakhtiyar.'

'Where is your mother, Mr Karan?'

'With your mother.'

'Just like the two of us together,' she said, gazing into Karan's deep blue eyes.

'But, I am indeed sorry! What was your mummy like?'

'I don't even know what my mother looked like.'

Karan became upset.

'She died just as I was born.'

'Whenever I recall my mother's face . . .' At the top of the stairs, she stopped, a little dizzy.

'When I recall . . .'

She wiped her tears with her handkerchief.

'I . . .'

She put her right hand on Karan's shoulder for support.

'I . . .'

She closed her eyes and fainted into Karan's arms.

The delicate scent of her white-rose powder, her halting heartbeat, the rapid rise and fall of her chest, her curls scattered across her wan face, and the isolated corners and polluted silences of Aaraam Gah's dusty atmosphere—all of these sent Karan into a daze.

Scattering clouds rained drops of water on Zahra's unconsciousness.

Zahra's eyes slowly fluttered open.

'Ms Bakhtiyar!?'

Karan continued to hold Zahra in his arms.

'My name is Zahra. You can call me Baby!'

'Ba . . . by!'

'Karan . . . No . . . What is your first name?'

'Mohan.'

'Mohan! A very handsome name! I will call you Mohan from now on.'

The haze that surrounded Mohan gradually dissipated into a dull yellow light from his past. His thoughts conjured up Aruni, his late uncle's youngest daughter, running around with joy, playing. He had loved Aruni greatly.

'You are lost in thought again.'

'I was thinking about Aruni. My cousin, Aruni. She used to call me Mohana, and I used to call her Baby.'

'But I am not your cousin. I am your girlfriend. Do you understand, my sweet white rose?'

Holding hands, they walked down the corridor and stopped in front of a door.

'I will tell Bobby and Fazlu to have the guest suite cleaned up today. It's been locked up for ages. This is the drawing room and the lounge, but you will take your meals with us. And this is your bedroom. You also have an interesting balcony. Come!'

The two of them went out on to the balcony.

'And this . . .' Zahra continued, 'this is the graveyard.'

Karan was stunned.

'Why is there a graveyard behind this "Aaraam Gah"?'

Several people were carrying a corpse down Dayal Bagh Road. Karan felt his hair stand up. For a moment, he imagined watching his own corpse being carried by the people down below. This guest house was becoming a symbol for what had become of his life. It was his compensation for trading away his blood . . . This dining room here, where he would be engrossed in the selection of extravagant and delicious food . . . And this ornate and elegantly decorated lounge where he would come to relax after having his meal. Just beyond the lounge was a delightful bedroom where his sleepy spirit would be entangled with Baby's breathing. And like a guilty conscience, he grew increasingly frightened seeing these terrifying dreams over and over. He would sleepwalk out of the bedroom and arrive out on the balcony. And this graveyard . . . He would leap down into the graveyard in his slumberous state!

'I am also terrified of this graveyard.'

Zahra rested her head on his shoulder.

'But Papa is rather strange. His conversations send shivers down one's spine.'

She slid even closer to Karan.

'Yesterday, he told me that he is convinced that Mother gets out of her grave and comes here daily. That she joins us for dinner. When he starts to smoke, she snatches the cigar from his fingers. The things he says are so haunting . . .'

She has sidled up as close to Karan now as possible.

'Mo—han!

The way she intoned the 'han' was like that first enticing bite of her favourite orange ice cream and savouring the feel of it on her tongue, before letting it slip down her throat. At that moment, her fears disappeared.

'Have you ever had an encounter with a ghost?'

'Shall I show you one, Baby?'

'What?! Where?' The lovely bowl of orange ice cream slipped from Zahra's hands, and she turned, frightened, to look over at the graveyard.

'Here. Turn around. Look at my face!'

Zahra lifted her eyes to his face now, let out a soul-crushing scream, and fell down unconscious—this time, for real.

CHAPTER 9

There used to be a time when ghosts were known to be forever ready to serve their masters at the mere rubbing of a lamp, and as a result, they were considered so harmless that even children would befriend them. But it was different these days. These days, one had to promise good payment to bring a ghost into one's service. Once they were employed, they would even tear out the stars from the firmament, and drop them at the feet of their masters.

Karan, too, once he was set up in Dr Bakhtiyar's guest house, was full of such harmless wishes, and once Zahra realized this, she laughed at the truth of that day when, terrified, she had lost control of her senses.

'What happened to me that day?'

'A delusion,' Dr Rana explained to Zahra. Dr Rana was visiting to carry out the blood transfusion for Dr Bakhtiyar with Karan's blood. 'Human beings have this capacity of deluding ourselves into believing things even when our conscious mind knows it is impossible.'

'But, doctor . . .' Karan began to speak. 'At that moment, I felt exactly as though I wasn't a human, that I was a ghost.'

'Well, Mr Karan, I can assure you that ghosts don't contain a single drop of blood,' said Dr Rana, with a smile.

'As long as there is blood in your veins, you will remain human.'

Though Dr Rana's remark carried no additional meaning, Karan turned serious at the significance of what he had just heard. Seeing Karan's change of expression, the doctor looked deeply apologetic.

'Mohan!' Zahra jumped in, in an effort to lighten the mood of the conversation.

'An extremely interesting English film is about to be released today, *Way to End the Whole World*. Would you accompany me to it, please?'

Dr Rana smiled and started to collect his things so that he could leave these two alone and join 'the whole world' somewhere far away.

In Aaraam Gah, Karan had every luxury imaginable. His health remained at its best despite donating blood occasionally. And yet, all his new-found luxuries could not do anything to abate his stress and mental crisis. This is what always befalls poor and sensitive individuals once they have tasted luxury. The surfeit of material goods transforms him into an unrecognizably covetous person and he begins to curse the very actions that supplied him with all these material comforts in the first place. The fear of their former poverty intensifies and adds to their distress even further.

Ultimately, Karan became accustomed to playing hide-and-seek with his mental crisis. Zahra's unexpected, westernized mannerisms and characteristics drew him in and Karan was completely taken with her. He spent most of his time with her—going to the cinema, clubs or to the horse-racing track. It was then that he began drinking alcohol regularly.

'Dev!'

Zahra had taken to addressing Karan by new and more affectionate names. Instead of 'Mohan', she would call him by these names, only to rankle him. What if the names belonged to her former lovers? What if the memories of these admirers stabbed her heart like broken thorns? Or perhaps, all these names represented a repeated single pleasure.

'Dev!'

'I am not Dev, Zahra.'

Even in his drunken state, his hide-and-seek with his own feelings continued.

'Dev is your father. I am just a tiny, beautiful parrot that your father, Dev, owns. Dev has the parrot's—what I mean is, the parrot is everything to Dev. That is why the very big Dev takes such care of the very little parrot . . .'

'Mohan! Mohan! Oh my God! You got tipsy so quickly!'

'Come, my *maina*, let me tell me you a story about a parrot and a Dev. I used to tell the same story to my

Aruni Baby. Come, Baby . . . Baby, you are also my
Aruni Baby. My . . . sister!'

'Don't mock me! Look, everyone is looking at us.
Let's go!'

Every once in a while, Karan would dress up in his
nicest suit to pay Bebe a visit.

Though Bebe had cautioned him repeatedly against
working for Dr Bakhtiyar, the uninhibited sincerity of
her own voice scared her into silence, lest Karan abandon
the idea entirely of working for Dr Bakhtiyar. It wasn't
that Bebe was happy to see him leap head first into the
dark well of death, but she also did not want him to lose
a job he had gotten with great difficulty.

'How long can a man sit idly, unable to find any
other work?' Bebe thought to herself. 'And, Karne
always assures me that there is no danger to one's life
from giving blood.'

Bebe considered Karan to be her own blood. But
even if she would have forbidden her own son from
taking this job, in her heart she would want him to
ignore her.

Because, although he loved Bebe dearly, he had
felt extremely worried that she would actually agree to
accompany him when he had requested her to move
with him to Aaraam Gah. His main fear was that her
coarse and unpolished behaviour would embarrass him
in front of the Bakhtiyar household.

'At this juncture of my life, I want to greet my own
death in peace, Karne. My bier must be carried away from

this very house. You should carry on, son. Just come to visit your poor old mother whenever you get a chance.'

'What do you mean "when I get a chance"? I will definitely come once or twice a week, at least. And Bebe, let the work at Ramjas's house go to hell.'

But Bebe didn't let the work at Ramjas's house go to hell.

'He's a very good boy. But who knows, he may turn his back on me. What will I do if ever that happened?'

But Karan didn't turn his back on her. Once every ten or fifteen days, he would set out for Bebe's house, with a basket of fruits, or with a bundle of clothes for her. On one occasion, he even had a gold ring made for Bebe.

'Wait, betaji.'

Of late, Bebe had taken to calling Karan 'betaji'. She used to call Ramjas's son 'betaji' as well, and her Karna was earning more than Ramjas's son after all.

'Betaji, why would you buy a ring for a wretched old woman like me? Now you tell me, Khubchand's mother, am I not too old to be wearing gold jewellery?'

The old woman's dirty, wrinkled finger shimmered with the joy of a new gold ring. The despondent part in an old mother's hair was being filled with vermilion from her son's earnings. She could not keep herself from laughing.

'Fine, betaji, if this makes you happy, I won't hurt you by refusing your gift.'

'Bhagwati's mother, look at this material for my tunic, and look at this new dupatta. My son Karna brought them. He works for some famous doctor, for three hundred rupees a month.'

Bebe had made Bhagwati's mother listen to this over and over as if she were trying to arrange a marriage between Karan and Bhagwati.

'That's fine, Bebe. But I've heard that his boss gives him three hundred rupees in exchange for his blood.'

Bebe hung her head in shame.

'Listen, betaji.'

She told Karan, 'Work as hard as you can to serve the boss. But do avoid this business of blood.'

She wiped her eyes with the corner of her hem. 'Even the fortunate are brought to tears on seeing how the poor live.'

'Bebe . . .' For the past several times, when he visited Bebe, he had been quite drunk.

'Happiness and sadness are all in God's hands. Aren't we happy as well as sad at the same time? Sometimes grief laughs, Bebe, and sometimes happiness sheds tears. My Bebe, this is all the mystery of God's ways. What can an unfortunate human do against that?'

Bebe, as if listening to a religious guru, sat enraptured. When Karan had stopped speaking, she rubbed her eyes, folded her hands and said, 'Jai Shri Krishan. What was the name of that Panditji Maharaj? I just had his name on the tip of my tongue, and I've already forgotten, his ideas were very pure, much like yours.'

'Bebe, ideas don't change anything. Actions bring change in the world. If an action is sinful, no amount of good thinking will make the outcome fruitful.'

Bebe, who had been sitting all this while with her hands folded and eyes closed, now opened them halfway and looked at Karan.

'Fine, betaji. Let me quickly make you some rotis.'

'No, Bebe.'

'What do you mean, "no"? Today, I've cooked your favourite—mashed eggplant.'

She leapt up to get her large brass plate and began cleaning it.

'You only come occasionally, now. Won't you at least eat from your Bebe's favourite plate?'

'It's not that, Bebe.' Karan's heart melted.

'The doctor's daughter refuses to eat without me.'

'There are thousands of girls out there.'

The newly cleaned brass plate shone like a mirror. But Bebe, who was used to scrubbing the dishes for others, kept on cleaning it.

'But there is only one Bebe, betaji.'

'No, Bebe. That girl is not an ordinary girl. She's very unusual, a gentle woman . . .'

However, not wanting to seem like he were inconsiderate of Bebe's feelings, he hesitated, and did not continue resisting.

Before he left, he usually gave Bebe ten, or sometimes, even twenty rupees.

'I still have some left from last time, betaji.'

She took the money and tied it up in her pallu, as was her habit.

* * *

'Namaste, sir.'

Karan would run into Hakeem Sukh Chen outside Bebe's house occasionally.

'Namaste, Karanji. Kha . . . kha . . . khoo!'

Despite his cough, there was the sound of a young man's passionate vitality in Hakeem Sukh Chen's voice.

'Please, don't go without partaking of the celebratory sweets.'

'Is there happy news?'

Karan was looking at him when a calf came running down the lane towards the Hakeem.

'Get out of here, you bastard!' the Hakeem yelled at the vagrant calf, swinging his cane around with great strength.

'Yes, Karanji, God has given me a son. Come, I have sweets for you inside.'

'Congratulations!'

What must a single man feel upon hearing the news of his child being born from the womb of another man's wife? Should he feel what a legitimate father would— completely overwhelmed by an excess of love for his newborn child, and ponder his own immortality? Or would this newborn child become his father's burden— a weight that would continue to increase as he carried it on his straining waist for his whole life? Karan's visage appeared simultaneously to darken and brighten.

'Heartiest of congratulations, sir!'

'No, my younger brother.'

To a happy man, every other man is an older or younger brother.

'I cannot let you be so formal. You must come inside and take the sweets I've set aside for you.'

Karan now found Hakeem Sukh Chen very affable.

'This man is my child's father. My child will jump around, make cooing noises, delight in the sounds of laughter and squeal louder as he plays on this man's chest. This man will buy toys and boxes of sweets for my child. My child!'

Karan's mind was reignited on imagining this new bud with his face. He felt his heart melt. The tight knots that had once developed in his mind about Ragini slackened. Now he found her quite admirable. Every woman, upon becoming a mother, is transformed into an individual deserving respect.

'Come, Karanji, won't you? The house feels so lonely without my wife and child. They will be back in a month or two.'

Karan followed the Hakeem into his house.

'Karanji, I am troubled by your job. You have to work hard and on top of that, you have to give away your blood. Even a bagful of money would not make up for this. That money remains a burden.'

A simple man's heart, absorbed in his own happiness, becomes very tender and he genuinely begins to feel the pain of others.

'I am very troubled!'

CHAPTER 10

Passion grew slowly in times long ago. From the first signs of consciousness, love began to bud and blossom, and secretly, internally, it moved through several phases before emerging entirely. Lovers would spend years on end securing their relationships with laughter, tears, and alternating between fear and joy, creating a durable feeling, and their relationships started to feel more complete, the bonds between them growing so strong that it became impossible to imagine being separated. In tiny alleys, paths, fields and gardens, the length and breadth of a couple's connection would comprise their entire lives. Till, at the end of time, the graves of the two companions would sit next to each other until their bones, in the studio of the earth, became the same composition.

But those were tales of the old days, when boulders and mountains had never moved. They rested their heads on the breasts of wistful valleys and slept while they saw lush, virginal dreams, and life had a firm foundation, immovable and completely at peace. In such conditions, human relations gradually began to flourish. And as they did, they became immensely strong, and their lives grew very long, immeasurable even, but these days, it was different. Today, life speeds along extremely rapidly in an electric train, and mountains, boulders, valleys and homes—all appear to be galloping alongside. And if it is difficult to observe static objects, then why not stop the train to look at them at the risk of being late?

In our hurried lifestyles, for one man and one woman to be perfectly suited to one another and tie the knot so quickly—and then quickly, while shedding their clothes, decide to go their separate ways, pretending to not even have spotted each other—the question of love never arises.

'Mohan! Mohan!'

In Aaraam Gah, Zahra's voice raced ahead of her to reach Karan's office first.

'My passport is finally ready.'

'Passport?'

Karan was writing out a note to one of Dr Bakhtiyar's medical suppliers.

'Oh right, your passport.'

'Look at this. Uncle Fazlu just brought it. Just look!'

Karan took the passport and began examining it.

'Oh, I'm so happy!'

Zahra came up behind Karan and draped her arms over his shoulders. She was already picturing herself disembarking at the London airport.

'Height: five feet, six inches; hair: black; eyes: dark brown.'

As he read the contents of Zahra's passport, a weird realization struck him that Zahra's description fit Shobha very closely. Karan had met Shobha a few times at a nightclub.

'Baby, let's go to the City Night Club tonight.'

'No, Mohan. This evening I am going shopping with Papa. I don't have much time before my departure.' Then, with a smile, she said, 'How wonderful! London is the gateway to all the world's culture. How wonderful!'

Zahra bent down to Karan's open mouth, as if, right now, it were the very gate to all the world's culture, and kissed him hard.

'Once I leave, what will you do, you poor boy? I am feeling a little sorry for you.'

'I . . . I . . .'

Karan had long decided that if Zahra was busy, he would just go to the City Night Club by himself that evening. He was sure to meet Shobha there today.

'I had a boyfriend, Mr Karan. He was very smart, exactly like you.' At their very first meeting, Shobha's voice had taken on a flirtatious lilt while talking to Karan.

'I find myself thinking about my boyfriend often whenever I am alone.'

'Oh, my poor Mohan! How I pity you! You have become very sad, haven't you? But I am very happy today, Mohan! You should be happy for me, too.'

'I am very happy, Baby. London really is a kind of paradise. Young men there really like the dark, dreamy eyes of Asian girls.'

'Really! Oh no! You are kidding!'

The dark glow of Zahra's eyes appeared heavy with sleep.

'No, Baby.'

The mysteries of Zahra's sleepy eyes had worked their magic on Mohan.

'You are like thunder. I swear, I still have not been able to grasp you. If you weren't going to England, then I . . . I . . .'

'What?'

'I'd marry you.'

He had blurted that out only to complete his sentence. And as soon as he had said it, the spell of those dreamy eyes shattered and vanished.

'Then I should definitely run away to England! Immediately! Right now!'

Zahra sat down heavily on to a nearby chair.

'You know, I hate marriage! I love my mother very much except for this. Why did she have to marry Papa?'

Karan began to laugh at this observation.

'If your mother hadn't married your father, how would you have been born, Baby?'

'How would I have been born?' Zahra fixed Karan with a pitiful gaze. 'How old-fashioned! Had you studied biology properly, you would know that marriage is not necessary to produce children.'

Karan was once again overcome with raucous laughter. To demonstrate his deep interest in the topic, he lit a cigarette, slowly and deliberately. He had become a chain-smoker now.

'There is a dangerous audacity in your ideas, Baby.'

'I'm not being audacious, Mohan. You're just old-fashioned. In the olden days, the idea of one man and one woman became the norm only because a woman only ever had the opportunity to meet one man, and a man, only one woman. Life was restricted to a tiny cell.'

Zahra didn't care much for cigarette smoke, but now that she was thrilled by her own passionate voice, she lit a cigarette for herself.

'We were trapped in the torments of this imprisonment of our small lives. If five to ten men could be made available, a woman could easily select two or three from among them. But if she only met one man her entire life, what kind of choice would the poor wretch have? A man might very well dream of hundreds or thousands of rupees, but ask a poor man if he'd like to own any, and he would joyfully accept even a single rupee. For a beggar who has a singular concern with his lack of wealth, a single rupee will be his entire universe! Folks from that time were like that old beggar, Mohan!'

'And modern folks?' Karan asked.

'Modern men and women are in contact with each other on a daily basis. Every moment, a new face . . . so why get married and bore yourself with the same face every day? In fact, the idea of marriage no longer fits in with our society.'

A new thought was dawning on Karan. Maybe, when human relations started developing at first, the wise must have seen the bond of marriage as unavoidable for the proper institutionalization of those relations. But today, as relationships have evolved endlessly, there is no longer a need for any institution.

'What else is a marriage but swearing oaths to gods and prophets?' Zahra said.

'Modern people have a much larger base of knowledge. They themselves have become gods and prophets with all that knowledge at their fingertips. So why debase this knowledge by swearing oaths to gods? No matter what kind of oath it is, an oath is demeaning. And so, I don't want to fall in my own estimation by getting married.'

'But Baby, the prophets and gods have infused our relations in spirit.'

Karan's thoughts, disturbed by possibilities, now steadied themselves before taking over his tongue.

'And it is because of the devotion and sanctity that our relationships have endured many pitfalls. Today our relationships are forged quickly and they break down just as easily.'

'They are forged quickly, true. But each moment is treasured and savoured like a gift. In the ancient days, there was no basis on which to forge a relation. One fell in a love with a man in secret, and before a relation could even be established, a bottle of poison was swallowed. I curse this type of love.'

'What are you two arguing about?'

The two of them turned towards the door in the direction of Dr Bakhtiyar's wheezing voice.

'Baby was speaking very passionately today, Dr Bakhtiyar.'

'It's true; my daughter enjoys her impassioned oratory.'

Dr Bakhtiyar spread himself out on a sofa in one corner of the room.

'Whomever she marries will have to forget about hot meals prepared at home, and will instead have to fill his stomach with her discourses.'

'We were just discussing the issue of marriages. Baby's views are extremely progressive.'

'I keep telling her that she is wasting her time going to England. She should become a leader in the women's movement here. The poor things are so illiterate. The work is virtuous, and one can make a name for oneself.'

'Stop that. You look at everything from your own viewpoint. Look, my passport has arrived.'

Zahra picked up the new passport and brought it to her father.

"There was a phone call from the ministry that the passport was ready. I sent Fazlu Uncle for it.'

Dr Bakhtiyar took the passport and said, 'Baby, go and tell Bobby to give me my multivitamin pill.'

'Hold off on the pill, Papa. First, look at my passport.'

'It's only a passport.'

But then to placate his daughter, he began examining its laminated pages.

'This photo of yours is flawless.'

He paused briefly as he gazed at Zahra's photo in the passport.

'All of your photos turn out so nicely.'

'Yes.'

Karan spoke, 'That day the proprietor of the pharmacy was totally taken by Baby's photo album. He wanted Baby to be the model for his posters.'

'If I want to be a model, Mohan, I will be a model for a German painter.'

'Our friend Yusuf is also a very talented painter, Baby. Why don't you model for him?'

'So what if he's had a few exhibitions?' Zahra replied to her father. 'That poor man is practically starving. In Europe, every painting sells for thousands of pounds. Mohan, remember that picture of me dressed up as a banana seller? I still have that costume saved. I will wear it in Europe to model for a famous painter and I will earn at least three thousand pounds. When Ms Henry Long signed her first Hollywood acting contract, she only received three thousand dollars. That was how the poor girl was initially exploited. But now she earns a full fifty thousand.'

Dr Bakhtiyar was amused by his daughter's childish ideas.

'You think that this is a joke, Papa? I am telling the truth. A full fifty thousand! But the poor girl signed her first contract for a mere three thousand. She bought a diamond necklace with that three thousand. I will buy a diamond necklace with my first earnings as a model, too, Papa!'

'Sure. Yes. Definitely.'

Dr Bakhtiyar removed a pipe and some tobacco from his pocket and continued to smile.

'Now go and tell Bobby to bring my multivitamin pill.'

'Wait, Papa. Can't you forget about your medicines just once? Mohan, I've saved that banana-seller costume carefully. When I won first prize in the fancy-dress show, I immediately decided that I would wear this when I modelled for some European painter. A woman selling bananas. Just think, Mohan, just think what a unique impression this will make on the European mind . . . How exciting, Papa . . .!'

'You will make two thousand five hundred pounds dressing up as a fake banana seller, Baby.'

Karan softened his tone to reduce the bitterness of his words. 'Meanwhile, the women who actually sell bananas can sell them for an entire day and not even earn two and a half rupees.'

'You are a blockhead! You were once a literature student, but you still haven't understood that in the fine arts, a successful imitation is worth a thousand times more than the real thing. A woman selling bananas is merely a woman selling bananas, but an artist is not trying to sell bananas or waste his valuable life for a mere two and a half rupees.'

'My father was a Hindi poet, Baby.'

Karan's thoughts raced back to his childhood, to grab hold of his father's finger.

'He was a very good artist, but art never let him even earn two and a half rupees.'

'He was a Hindi poet, after all! If I were in his shoes, I would have written in English and I would have given the copyright for my works to a British publisher. Instead of writing poetry in the language of a country that cannot even take a break from selling bananas, it would be better if poets started selling bananas, too.'

'Okay, Baby. Now go and tell Bobby to bring my multivitamin.'

'Oh! how boring! O . . . kay, Papa! But, first you have to promise me something. Then I will go.'

'What kind of promise?'

'That you will take me shopping this evening. There are only a few days left until my departure. If I don't get to England by next month, my admissions will be cancelled.'

'Okay.'

'Be ready at 6.30 p.m. And don't even try to pretend that you are sick!'

When she had left, Dr Bakhtiyar turned to face Karan.

'She's quite flighty and talkative, isn't she?'

'Yes, sir. She can never sit quietly. Even when I imagine her in my mind, her mouth is moving rapidly. She just keeps talking and talking.'

'Once Baby leaves us, Aaraam Gah will be as quiet as a graveyard. I . . . I am afraid that I will pass away before she returns.'

'No, you are worrying unnecessarily. You will be in perfect health.'

'I have another fear,' Dr Bakhtiyar said as he looked into Karan's eyes. 'That you will leave as well, once Baby is gone.'

'What are you talking about? I will always serve you with sincerity.'

For a moment, Karan mused on asking Dr Bakhtiyar for a raise.

'Doctor Sahib, I came here to serve you. Baby leaving does not affect our arrangement in any manner,' he assured.

Karan was wondering about calling Shobha to ask her to meet him at the City Night Club later that evening.

'What I mean is, as long as Baby is here, you shall find this lonely place attractive, entertaining. But once she leaves . . .'

'Have a little faith in my loyalty, doctor sahib . . . My goodness! I completely forgot! The laboratory sent over the results of your medical tests. Here, have a look!'

Dr Bakhtiyar leapt up in great urgency and took the medical result sheet from Karan.

'Haemoglobin, 35 per cent . . . Uff!'

He looked over at Karan.

'It's low! . . . And look, my blood pressure is worse . . . And emphysema . . . The doctors are apprehensive that

I may also suffer from emphysema . . . Kh-cough . . .
Khoo . . . Did you hear me coughing? An emphysema
patient coughs exactly like that. How will I be able to
have my gall bladder operation in this condition?'

'Don't worry, doctor sahib. You will get better soon.
Your allergies have dropped from twenty to a mere
thirteen per cent. After the operation, the other issues
will also resolve themselves.'

'My boy, the operation is the problem. If these other
issues remain, there is no way for me to have the operation.
I am not foolish enough to be scared irrationally. I have
spent my entire life doing exactly this work.'

'Don't worry so much'

'How can I not worry? If I don't have the operation
soon, my condition will deteriorate. Even with a steady
supply of your blood, my haemoglobin levels are low. It's
all very strange.'

'Papa, Bobby has gone out somewhere,' Zahra said
entering the room.

'So, what should I do about that?'

'Being ill has made you very irritable, Papa. Here are
your multivitamin pills.'

'I won't take any more damn pills—Call Dr Rana
and ask him to come over immediately! I . . . My . . .'

Zahra looked over at Karan in confusion.

'The laboratory sent over his medical sheet today. He
didn't like what he read.'

'You are very strange, Papa! How does this medical
sheet matter? You were fine just a few minutes ago.'

'Baby, I am not fine. How many times have I told you that I am not fine. You just want to celebrate like it's Eid. You want to go to England happily, and one day you will receive a telegram informing you of my death. I am telling you I am seriously ill.'

'So you won't go shopping with me?'

'No. Karan, call Dr Rana. I am going upstairs to my bedroom.'

'Then write me out a cheque for two thousand rupees, Papa. I will go with Mohan.'

'You are only concerned about shopping while I am over here dying . . .'

Muttering, Dr Bakhtiyar got up to leave the room.

'Two thousand rupees . . .' Zahra pursued him.

'Hello!'

Karan dialled the number.

'Ms Shobha, please? What?! Wrong number?!'

Karan replaced the receiver.

'Damn it! I dialled the number for Dr Rana and asked for Ms Shobha. I have become such an ass!'

CHAPTER 11

Zahra had just left for England.

With his eyes fixed on the airplane, Karan felt as if his sins had grown wings and taken flight, crossing oceans, vanishing from his sight.

It is true that neither sins nor virtues have their own recognizable visages. Nevertheless, both good and evil have been presented to humanity in the form of recognizable faces. Our religion, literature and history contain never-ending stories of good and evil taking forms. Should the epics depicted in the caves of Ajanta be defaced, the fabric of a great culture, founded on principles of reward and punishment, would be shredded. In truth, our ability to reason and understand becomes ineffective and unreliable without faces to connect it to. Without faces, sin and virtue become indistinguishable.

A few days before Zahra's departure, Karan began to believe that Zahra was a living, breathing embodiment of his sins. She had turned into a

125

manifestation of his primal desires and trying to satisfy them had made his head spin, had shoved him off the fixed highways of life. He began to think of beautiful women as mere instruments of pleasure. And by now, he had become breathless, chasing after them over and over. He wanted to admit defeat. He wanted to rest so that he could contain the remaining goodness inside of him. He wanted to stare his sadness in the eye with its own eyes brimming with kindness, and he wanted to restore its trust all over again. When such secret desires take form inside the heart of a sinner, then in days, or weeks, they begin to feel enormous— like they would to an innocent virgin. And he, as if he were watching his own daughters come of age, would suddenly be transformed. The sparkle of sin would now seem nauseating to him.

When Karan saw his sin, Zahra, fly off and vanish into the vast expanse, he breathed a sigh of relief. Who knew why or from whence Bele Rina, lost and forgotten, came and stood on the threshold of the temple of his mind saying:

'Thank the son of God that I have found you. Just look at the blisters on my feet from my never-ending search for you. I have knocked on countless doors. My heart promised me that we would surely meet. Here, look. Look at me here!'

Karan stepped forward and embraced this incarnation of goodness. He was neither desperate nor smiling, nor crying. Drowning in the wild vortex, polluted with sin, he was now buoyed by moonlight. He was finally headed towards a safe harbour where complete peace was to be his.

'Let's go, brother.'

The boundless sky swallowed Zahra's airplane. Dr Bakhtiyar spoke very wistfully and dejectedly to Karan, his face sullen. As if he had stepped into life's hazy light, just before descending into the darkness of death.

'Let's go. Let's go to Aaraam Gah.'

'Please. Let's.'

'Yes, sir. Let's go now,' said one of Zahra's boyfriends, Mazhar. But his eyes were still raised up to the empty heavens. Perhaps he could see several girls in the expanse.

Qamar, Shelly, Zahra.

Each in their turn, first swinging close to him, and then flying off far away—farther and farther. Becoming mere specks. And then even these specks vanished.

'Won't you say hello?'

Mazhar sidled up closer to one of Zahra's girlfriends who had come to the airport to see her off.

'When the distance between us grows so great,' Karuna asked Mazhar as she thought of Zahra, 'why can't we see each other?'

'Because that is what God wills.'

He took Karuna off to the side.

'The eyes that God gives are only able to see things that are close by.'

'That's why you've stayed so far from me these last few months, right?'

The two of them dashed off for coffee.

Karan's heart and soul were still completely affixed to thoughts of Bele Rina.

'Every human being has one love, one Bele Rina. His one exalted, pure angel, who never left him, no matter where she was now. Her recognizable musical signature is always nearby.'

'Drive quickly, brother.'

Dr Bakhtiyar and Dr Rana returned to the motor car, and Dr Rana turned to Karan and called out to him. Karan was walking very slowly, his head drooping.

'When I went to England,' Dr Rana said climbing into the back seat with Dr Bakhtiyar, 'the flight took two whole days. But these days, the Boeing gets you there in a few hours.'

'True.'

Dr Bakhtiyar responded disinterestedly, 'In this age, everything moves at a very rapid pace, doctor sahib.'

Karan sat in the seat next to the driver.

'This Boeing airplane flies at the speed of sound.'

'But Mr Karan,' Dr Bakhtiyar's impudent driver couldn't hold his tongue, 'this must be the kind of sound only rich people make so that it can go so far in mere moments. The sounds that we poor folk make can go only a few metres before they are punctured.'

'You have been warned repeatedly, Fazlu,' Dr Bakhtiyar said, pretending to be angry. 'Don't stick your nose where it doesn't belong.'

Fazlu turned on the ignition, as if to say, 'What's eating you, Baba? You are the lord only for a few more days, maybe months. In God's kingdom, the rich and the poor are all equal.'

But this time, he stayed silent and he drove the motor car out of the parking space. And as the vehicle began travelling smoothly on the paved street, Fazlu turned this thought over and over in his head.

'Once we are reduced to ashes, we are both equals. But then, what's the point of equality when you're turned to ash? The real fun would be if we were actually equal while we were alive.'

The motor car matched the pace of Fazlu's daring and exciting thoughts.

'Doctor, I wanted . . .' Dr Bakhtiyar said to Dr Rana, 'I wanted Baby to stay here. Right now, my health . . . I have lost all my confidence.'

'You are needlessly getting upset, doctor sahib. I am not even sure how to explain things to you, you yourself being a renowned doctor. Your minor illnesses are merely temporary. The biggest issue is your gall bladder. And that, God willing, will be much better after the operation.'

'How will it ever get better? Improvement can only happen after the operation, right? But do you think that my health can withstand the stress of an operation? I am convinced that I will die as soon as the anaesthetic is administered.'

'You are being unnecessarily pessimistic.'

'I am not a pessimist, doctor. This concern has arisen from knowledge and experience. At the beginning of the year, you delayed my operation even though my haemoglobin levels were quite good, and my blood pressure and emphysema were not as bad.'

'Don't worry, doctor sahib. You will definitely get better.'

'What do you mean "better"? The high blood pressure is killing me. When I get chest pains, I feel like putting a noose around my neck. I was so scared that I didn't even want to have my gall bladder X-rayed. As long as I didn't know I had the disease, at least I did not worry so much.'

Karan really wanted to scold the old geezer for his senseless blathering. But he merely turned away, and, with a gentle smile, said, 'An X-ray has to be performed.'

The great Fazlu's pampered imagination galloped along, increasing its speed along with the speed of the car. 'Look at how much our daktar fears death. The poor man dies so many deaths from fear before he actually dies. I have had a hundred illnesses, but here he is, crying and wailing. This moron makes such a fuss about his temporary illnesses that he breeds even more of them. So why shouldn't they love him back?'

'Can I say something, master? You have made your illnesses greater in your own mind than they actually are.'

'Why don't you just stay quiet?'

This time, Dr Bakhtiyar's anger was real.

'H-h-h-ey! Do you want to crash into the bridge?'

Fazlu very expertly turned the steering wheel and barely saved the car from a dangerous situation.

'Teetar Shah's curve is very precarious.'

When Fazlu's breathing returned to normal, he said, 'Damn, I come this way every single day.'

'Come now, drive more carefully,' Dr Rana consoled him.

'If the car were to fall off the bridge, do you know what would have happened?' Dr Bakhtiyar was still panting.

'What would have happened?'

Fazlu retorted, 'Why do we even need to know what happens after death?'

He started to smile. 'What would have happened?'

A vision flashed before Dr Rana's eyes, of his wife sitting by the head of his corpse and wailing mournfully. He loved his wife very much. Suddenly, his corpse sat up and wiped his wife's tears. Then he saw his wife's brothers consoling her. He hated his brothers-in-law deeply.

'Doctor sahib, you have spoilt your driver. Even when you scold him, he just smiles and ignores you. If something really were to happen, what is it that would have happened?'

'What would have happened—?' Karan thought. 'That death would have been better than my present abstract death. To die once and for all was better than this gradual suicide.'

'Master, how far has Baby's airplane gone by now?' Fazlu thought of Zahra and he couldn't keep quiet.

'Pay attention to your driving, man.' Dr Rana spoke in a stern tone, 'Or you will be the end of all of us.'

Saying which, he turned to address Dr Bakhtiyar. 'What subject does Babyji plan to write her PhD thesis on?'

'On the demons in the Ramayana.'

The doctor chuckled at what he considered his daughter's illogical choice.

'On the demons in the Ramayana? That is a very interesting topic. But why to go all the way to England to study that?'

'Baby wanted to write about a British poet,' Karan interjected. 'But the professor at the English university advised her to undertake an Indian project instead. One day, in a conversation I suggested this topic in complete jest, but to my surprise Baby liked it. And in her acceptance letter, the professor was endlessly enthusiastic.'

'But wouldn't the resources available here be much more authentic and helpful for writing this thesis?'

'Baby was adamant to get her PhD from an English university.'

'What a completely absurd topic.' Dr Bakhtiyar stopped himself from laughing out loud.

'It would be better if she got married and settled down rather than working on this ridiculous subject. The ghosts in the Ramayana . . . No, what was that word? . . . Right, demons.'

'The truth is that the English mind has reached the limits of its own culture and is now tired of it,' Karan said, sounding very philosophical. 'And having learnt from the barbarians and the Romans, the repressed British nature becomes powerless against a bestial sensibility. I am certain that Babyji's article will be much celebrated in the West.'

'But it is also necessary to be familiar with the context of this topic. How will Baby find any relevant material there?' Dr Rana wondered.

'She's probably never even looked at the Ramayana.'

'She will now,' Karan replied.

'There are thousands of such books in English in the British libraries. The poor British have never even read Valmiki in Sanskrit. Our students can always refer to these books if they are interested. And . . . then they talk to the British scholars and professors about these topics in a very knowledgeable manner, in an effort to be considered pandits or maulvis about Eastern culture.'

'Are you implying that the entire field of literary research is a bluff?'

'What else? They go there and start wearing Eastern turbans in order to impress them. Then, in order to impress us when they are back here, they . . .'

'Wear hats!' Dr Rana laughed in delight.

In a bit, the small party had arrived at Aaraam Gah. Dr Bakhtiyar and Karan alighted the car.

'Go,' Dr Bakhtiyar said to Fazlu. 'Drop Doctor Sahib off.'

'Where?'

Fazlu really disliked Dr Rana.

'To the graveyard!' Dr Rana snapped angrily, as he sensed Fazlu's displeasure.

'What do you mean?'

'Home, man. Home!'

'Yes, sir, I understand.'

Fazlu started the car with an intentional jolt. His turns were also unnecessarily sharp and uncomfortable.

Karan headed straight to his bedroom. He changed out of his clothes, stretched out on the bed, and stared up at the empty walls. He felt exhausted. He lay like this for quite some time.

His mind was full of the thoughts of his past. About Bele Rina . . . About his lost abilities . . .

An eerie breeze in from the graveyard wove nets made of rings upon rings of shadows in the room. The dead peered into the room, looking at him with wonder. He continued to remain completely still as if he had already died and his soul had gone to meditate on some quiet bank of the Ganges.

Perhaps a new human being was being built inside of him!

CHAPTER 12

'Doctor sahib!' Karan addressed the doctor in a very serious tone during breakfast the next morning.

'Hmph!' Dr Bakhtiyar replied very inconsiderately.

'I want to resign from my job.'

Shocked, Dr Bakhtiyar looked up at him.

'Doctor sahib, I can't bear to keep going against my conscience any longer . . . You aren't giving me a salary for my work, rather you are compensating me for my blood.'

'That's true.' Dr Bakhtiyar's tone grew angrier. 'But you knew that from the beginning. So why this new-found conscience suddenly?'

'I was desperate. But I can't keep doing this any longer.'

'I had my suspicions from the start. You wanted to take unethical advantage of my situation.' Dr Bakhtiyar's lips began to tremble in rage. 'You know, the doctor has ordered me to never get agitated. Let's settle the matter right now.'

'No, doctor sahib, you are misunderstanding me. I will continue to give you blood whenever you need it. But I won't sell my blood for money.'

This new twist took Dr Bakhtiyar by surprise even as his temper cooled a bit. He eyed Karan with suspicion. 'I . . .'

'No, you are deceiving me,' said Dr Bakhtiyar still not entirely sure of Karan's actual intentions. 'You really are incredibly shallow. With Zahra gone, you know that you are important to my well-being. And, you are taking advantage of that. Had you waited a few more days, I might have raised your salary myself.'

'No, doctor sahib. Please try to understand me. I am not going to sell my blood any more. Selling human blood really means bartering one's love and one's duty. This is the reason that I detest Sardar Bahadur Shamsher Singh, too. So how can I do the same thing? I will continue to take care of you and continue to give you my blood, but I cannot accept a salary for any of that.'

'But . . . But you must accept a salary for the other work you do, Karan,' Dr Bakhtiyar insisted. 'Just consider it your salary for the other duties you perform.'

'How can I? A lie is still a lie in any form, doctor sahib. It troubles me deeply that despite the work I do, I end up feeling like I don't deserve my salary.'

Dr Bakhtiyar put his cup of tea down on the table and looked at Karan with both admiration and curiosity. 'What is it that you are saying?'

'I don't want compensation for my moral obligation. You pay me three hundred rupees a month as salary in addition to food and accommodation. And we all know that all this is, in reality, the price of my blood and human obligations—my conscience—'

'Okay, don't bore me now,' Dr Bakhtiyar said, extending some porridge towards him. 'You are probably just hungry. A hungry man's conscience can trouble him excessively.'

'No, doctor sahib, I . . .'

'Come now. Let's drop this issue. We will deal with your salary later, and if you really want to work for free, what is it to me?' Dr Bakhtiyar smiled, shaking his head. 'You have picked a strange thing to dig your heels in on. People like you, with your heads all turned around, have driven the capitalists crazy. Just think, even as an employee in a welfare state, you would earn a hundred rupees, or maybe even more, doing the same work.'

'It's not an issue of money . . .'

'It is indeed an issue of money. But it is not your fault. You were, after all, born into a noble environment where people are content to subsist on dry bread alone when they do not get a decent meal. Or, instead of bread, they may even consider themselves blessed by God and live only on morals. However, if you are not really a hypocrite, then I applaud your values.'

He pulled his chair very close to Karan.

'Doctor sahib, I'm not saying this to be applauded for my feelings, but do try to understand the reality of the matter. I truly believe that a man who chases only the jingling of money loses all his humanity. He loses the ability to laugh with joy when he is happy or shed tears in sympathy with another's pain.'

Karan's voice took on an endearing impatience like that of a son being reunited with his long-lost father.

'Why won't you try and understand me?'

Dr Bakhtiyar really did find pearls, diving into Karan's blue eyes.

'Karan, you are as dear to me as my own son.'

Patting Karan on the back, he continued, 'My own son, Rafi, my firstborn. He died when he was ten years old. Were he still alive, I would want him to be just like you.'

He wiped his tears and began to clean his glasses.

'Stand up for me, son. I want to take a good look at you.'

Obliging the sad old man, Karan stood up. Dr Bakhtiyar put his glasses back on and turned to look at him.

'This is the first time I've really looked at you. It's as if my forgotten, lost Rafi has suddenly returned to me . . . You are right. It is a sin to put a price on human feelings.'

Karan thought he heard the sounds of a wedding procession fill the deserted Aaraam Gah. Maybe all the corpses in the graveyard had put on their wedding finery and were dancing in Rafi's wedding procession.

'Sit down, son.'

Sitting under the shaded aegis of his father, the orphan boy began to transform into a prince.

'All these medicines have addled my brain. Karan, I believe you are right. One cannot set a price on blood. Human blood is a priceless pearl, so . . . So . . . I have come to the conclusion that I will no longer use your blood. Think about it, would I have ever purchased Rafi's blood if he were around . . .'

'No, doctor sahib . . .'

But a single thought brought him to a sudden halt. 'Did truly relevant relationships exist only through bonds of family—mother, father, brother, sister . . . a wife even? When people remain truly faithful to each other, then don't those who are not related also become family?'

'Don't you agree, Karan?'

Watching Karan lost in silent thought, Dr Bakhtiyar began again, 'What father wants to see his beautiful boy's body drained of its blood?'

'No, uncle!' Karan exclaimed, forging the first link in the chain of his relationship with Dr Bakhtiyar. 'It's the bottles of the People's Blood Bank that are drained . . . when a person gives his blood willingly his body glows, beaming with honour and beauty.'

'Ah! That is a wonderful observation, son! Despite having discovered all these medicines to fight human illnesses, I never thought of things the way you described them. How can human beings diagnose their happiness or satisfaction, indeed,' Dr Bakhtiyar added, as he stroked his belly. 'I still feel a slight twinge here, but, listening to you, I just realized how insignificant that pain was in the face of the pain the world suffers.'

'Yes, sir, I, too, had trouble understanding this fact.'

The room glowed with the enlightenment as if Gautama Buddha himself might have experienced meditating under an ancient tree in Gaya.

Until it finds the vast expanse of the blue sea to drown and lose itself into, an individual's own grief and pain cries out, writhing, complaining, like a river's current, never finding peace.

Karan looked at Dr Bakhtiyar's wan face.

'Uncle, a person can derive great comfort if he learns to drown his own sorrow in the sorrow of the world.'

'Master, has Babyji reached England?' Bobby was clearing the emptied teacups from the table.

'Yes,' Dr Bakhtiyar replied. 'Why? Are you sad about her leaving?'

'Yes, sir.' Bobby's face fell as he replied, 'Babyji was always calling me so loudly! Bobby! Bobby! And Bobby ran as soon as soon as he heard, sometimes here, sometimes there!'

Bobby demonstrated by running around a few paces, to explain what he meant.

Karan turned to Dr Bakhtiyar and said, 'Baby brought so much brightness into the house.'

'Yes.' Dr Bakhtiyar had been so lost in his thoughts, diving farther and farther into the ocean in search of pearls, that Karan's words drew him back like a man quickly returning to the surface to catch his breath. 'Just think about it. What silly reason to leave all of us to go to London . . .? The demons of the Ramayana?! Crazy girl.'

'Master, our Babyji's reasons might seem crazy to some,' Bobby interjected, as he paused what he was doing. 'But she isn't crazy. Instead, she drives even the biggest intellectuals crazy.' Bobby looked at Karan and smiled wide, baring all his teeth.

Karan turned to look at the portrait of a young Zahra that hung on the wall.

'This photo was taken,' Dr Bakhtiyar began, 'when Zahra was maybe seven or eight years old. She was very lovely. She was always by my side, squealing with delight. Daughters are usually totally taken with their mothers, but Baby was always mine.' Dr Bakhtiyar roared with laughter at a beautiful memory. 'But, she's completely different now. Just look at the condition she abandoned me in. Are daughters supposed to behave like this?'

'I will watch over you, uncle. Why are you so worried?'

'I am not worried. I know you shall take care of me. But am I completely wrong in thinking that no daughter should behave like this? Do they not have any obligations? Death is hovering over my head and the memsahib is flying, joyfully, to the land of demons . . . Bobby!' Agitated, Dr Bakhtiyar called to Bobby. 'Go and get my sleeping pills. Last night I was tossing and turning the entire time.' The trouble with his gall bladder had made Dr Bakhtiyar uncomfortable.

'Can I tell you something, doctor sahib?' Karan said sensing Dr Bakhtiyar's need to dive back into the ocean in search of pearls.

'Come on, say it already.'

'I want to volunteer with the free blood bank of the Social Service. You know that the free blood bank is always empty. If the public were to be made aware of the needs . . . what I mean is, if the movement for the free blood bank were organized in a systematic way, then . . .'

'Yes, yes, fine, now drop this subject, already! Why are you boring with me this? Do whatever you want to.'

Karan had just come out of his own reverie, so this snapping only made him smile, rather than anger him.

Meanwhile, Bobby placed the mixture of milk and sleeping pills before Dr Bakhtiyar. After gulping it down, Dr Bakhtiyar once again addressed Karan.

'Yes, your idea is actually a very good one. The movement for the free blood bank should begin immediately. It is the need of the hour.'

'Yes, sir, exactly . . .'

'Tell Dr Manga of the Social Service League that I will make a donation of five thousand rupees to the League for this movement.'

'Sir? . . . Thank you very much! You . . .'

'Fine, fine! Now let's end this discussion. I am going up to my bedroom.'

He took a few steps and stopped. 'In a few hours, we should be receiving the telegram informing us of Baby's safe arrival. It will be good if it comes.'

Once Dr Bakhtiyar had left, Karan turned to Bobby. 'Go and tell Fazlu Uncle to get the car ready. I need to go to the offices of the Social Service League.'

On the paved road, as the car sliced through the throngs of people and vehicles on its way to the offices of the Social Service League, Karan was busy imagining his conversation with Dr Manga.

'Doctor sahib, your blood bank needs to be so successful that all of the blood kept for sale in the commercial blood banks become unnecessary. I am prepared to work day and night until we succeed. I am willing to organize a publicity campaign so that the extra blood of healthy men and women can be of use to those in need, instead of fanning the flames of their baser instincts.

'Doctor sahib, our blood bank should have every blood type in very large quantities. I want to ensure that no doctor at any hospital ever has to worry that their patient might die from lack of availability of a rare blood type. No one should need to pay for blood. The Social Service League's free blood bank will shut down the warehouses of the traders of human blood.

'Doctor sahib, Dr Bakhtiyar has promised to donate five thousand rupees to your blood bank. I will also make requests to all of the well-to-do men in the city, convince them all to help the blood bank.

'Doctor sahib, take my blood today. Take Fazlu Uncle's blood as well. I will bring Bobby here tomorrow . . . .'

'Babu, you are lost in your thoughts,' said Fazlu as the car crossed over the Teetar Shah Bridge.

'Uncle, I'm going to give my blood!'

'What?!'

'He . . . ey! Careful. The car will head off the bridge.'

'Going to give your blood? To become a martyr?'

'No, uncle. Countless sick people have need of our blood. There is a bank here that collects blood.'

'A bank? For blood?'

'Yes, not for money, just to store human blood. This bank gives dying patients blood for free and saves their lives. It reminds me of the truth that every human has a right to their share of human blood. This blood bank is a reserve from which to draw their share of happiness, health, and to fulfil their needs. The children of Adam all belong to a single family, and members of this family should share equally in the joys and sorrows of all.'

'Babu, that was a fine speech, but tell me, is it really true . . .?'

'Yes, one hundred per cent.'

'Then I will give my blood, too. If these things are true, babu, then, absolutely, take all of my blood!'

As the Teetar Shah bridge shrank into the distance behind them, the bridge's cackles grew louder as it gazed upon the car for as long as it could.

At the offices of the Social Service League, Dr Manga was quite moved by Karan's enthusiasm.

'If we could get a few more volunteers like yourself, Mr Karan, we could turn this society around. I've just received a phone call from the hospital that they have a desperate need for type O, RH negative blood. But what can we do . . .'

'What blood type was that?'

'O negative.'

'That is my blood type. You can draw some immediately!'

Dr Manga rang the bell immediately.

'Nurse, take a pint of this man's blood right away, and have it sent to Janta Hospital. Mr Karan, there is a patient with your blood type who is lying unconscious, listening to the approaching footsteps of death. Perhaps now he might be saved.'

Karan beamed.

'Nurse, hurry up!'

'Yaas, daktar!'

Uncle Fazlu suddenly insisted, 'Take my blood, too! If I die, it will have been for nothing, but this way it can at least be of use to some poor man.'

When Karan and Fazlu returned to their motor car, their faces bore the kind of radiance that angels possess.

'Uncle, I'm very happy today.'

'I am, too, Karan Babu. I was delighted when I saw my blood flowing out of me. Like my strength was going to be reborn today!'

After the car had travelled some distance, it stopped suddenly, as if it wanted to hear more of their languid conversation.

'What's happened to the car?'

'It was bound to happen, uncle. The car is angry with us because it couldn't give blood and we could.'

'Now that's a strange thing to say, babu. But to tell you the truth, many times I've felt as if this car of mine is alive like you and me, and understands everything we say.'

'Then I am certain that it wants to give its blood, too.' Karan began to laugh.

The sixth or seventh time that Karan pulled on the starter, the car let out something like a scream, and, unexpectedly, began to run.

'I've saved a life today, uncle.'

'Yes, babu. Allah will protect your life as well!'

'Uncle, your blood won't go to waste, either. Perhaps your blood will bring a mother back her child, and overwhelmed by her sudden happiness, she will never stop laughing.'

Fazlu could not stop thinking about saving the life of that wailing mother's child, and suddenly, he burst into uncontrollable fits of laughter.

'Ha ha ha haa ha ha haa . . . haahaa . . .'

The motor car broke through one of the barriers of the Teetar Shah Bridge, tumbling approximately twenty feet down into one of the city's dirty canals, tumbling upside down.

CHAPTER 13

Fazlu was buried in the graveyard, and Karan lay unconscious, groaning, in Janta Hospital. He had multiple injuries, and the doctors suspected that he might have fractured his skull as well.

On the third evening, Karan's eyes opened halfway, just enough so that he saw, near his feet, the hazy image of Bele Rina, her clothes snowy white, her expression pained but merciful, angelic, a thin, courageous smile spreading across her face.

Karan wanted to sit up, but he couldn't. He felt as if nails had been hammered into his arms. He couldn't move. He smiled at Bele Rina, helpless and crestfallen, and then he began to whimper.

Bele Rina's faint smile brightened as she saw him regain consciousness. She moved over to the head of the bed and lovingly bent closer to him.

'Be . . . ele . . . Rina . . .!' The faintest of groans escaped Karan's quivering lips.

Bele Rina remained bent over him, smiling, to draw away his pain.

'B . . . ele . . . Rina, where . . . were . . . you?'

'You are much better.'

'Bele . . .'

'Now you need to shleep.'

Karan's heavy, half-opened eyes closed by themselves, but his lips kept moving as if they wanted to say 'Bele Rina' over and over.

On the fourth day, the effects of the morphine still lingered on Karan, but when Bele Rina arrived he called out to her.

'Bele Rina . . .!'

'Don't shpeak!'

Bele Rina stuck a thermometer under his tongue. She turned away from him and began reviewing the patient sheet.

'Bele Rina . . .!'

When Bele Rina removed the thermometer from his mouth, Karan wanted to lift his head up towards her.

'Bele Rina!'

Finally, her duties done, she bent over him and smiled.

'I am not Bele Rina. I am Julia.'

'Not Bele Rina?'

Karan closed his eyes. A few drops of water escaped the boiling cauldron.

'Okay, okay, why are you crying? I really am Bele Rina.'

Once again, he opened his eyes to look her over carefully.

'Fazlu . . . Uncle . . . how is he?'

'Phajloo?'

'Y . . . es . . . The one . . . car . . . he was driving . . . oh!'

The nurse made the sign of the cross over her chest and then kissed her fingertips.

'How is he . . . Uncle?'

'He is . . . He . . .'

But the nurse remained silent.

'What . . . Has he died?'

Karan heard the rumble of the low, dark clouds outside, and like an elderly guard at a deserted guest house, he closed his eyes tightly.

On the fifth day, the nurse was again hovering near Karan's bed.

'Your health is much improved today!'

'You are right. But you are also Bele Rina.'

The nurse placed his head in her lap and began to spoon drops of orange juice down his throat.

'Yes . . . I am both Julia and your Bele Rina, too.' She patted Karan's cheeks tenderly. 'Your health is improved today. Your temperature is normal.'

In between his muffled thanks fell the drops of life-giving orange juice.

'You are Bele Rina . . . Bele Rina . . . Bele . . . R . . .'

Had he not been depleted by exhaustion, he would have said, 'Bele Rina is the name given to the body that a spirit takes, a spirit that is committed to making another's pain its own, and whose own pain is unknowable . . . You are also my Bele Rina, Julia . . . My girlfriend . . . My light . . . You are my faith in the goodness of humanity. You sow your smiles into the chest of the damp earth . . . You hide your own tears in order to wash the vessels of happiness for others.'

After a little while, the doctor arrived.

'Hello!'

A very jovial man, he sat next to Karan and began to examine him.

When he noticed a drop of blood slowly seeping from Karan's nose, he gave a sideward glance to the nurse, a worried look. He gently inserted a needle into his arm.

'Did it hurt?'

'No,' Karan replied.

'Have you got the X-ray of his skull?' the doctor asked the nurse.

'No, it will come tomorrow.'

The doctor appeared concerned and took the nurse to one side. The two whispered for a few minutes. The doctor left and the nurse returned to Karan and gave him some sleeping pills.

'Is Uncle Fazlu dead?'

'Don't talk. The doctor says everything is fine.'

There was such tenderness in her manner.

That evening, as Karan lay on the bed staring at the wall, lost in some quandary that cut to his soul, he was suddenly shaken out of it by a familiar voice

'My son . . . Karne, my son!'

Bebe's loving, blind voice ran towards the doorway, bumping and clashing into everything in the room, resounding finally in Karan's ears.

'Bebe . . .!'

It was as if Bebe were kissing his wounds and dressing them.

'What have you done to yourself, Karne?'

'Bebe . . .!'

The son dropped all his cares into his mother's arms and began to laugh, to cry.

'Ramjas's son told me what happened today, otherwise how would an unfortunate wretch like me ever know? Memsahib!' Bebe called for Julia. 'My son will be all right, won't he?'

'Yes, everything will be fine.' Julia had put her hand on Bebe's shoulder and replied with much sympathy. Bebe felt as if the goddess Parvati were granting her a boon for a son.

'Don't worry, mother. I will take care of your son.'

In her mind, Bebe folded her hands and bowed to the goddess Parvati. She suddenly remembered that the priest at the Shiv temple had asked for her brass plate for the evening prayer last Monday.

'Maharaj!' Bebe had folded her hands and beseeched the priest. 'Take my life, but don't take this plate. Every event in my life is drawn on that plate. If you take this plate from me, I will have nothing to remember my life by.'

The priest had been very angry.

'I should give this plate to the priest,' Bebe now thought. 'Perhaps this is the reason for Karne's tragedy.'

'Mother!' Julia was trying to get Bebe up from Karan's bed. 'You can go and sit in the chair over there. Your son really needs to rest.'

'Yes, memsahib.'

She folded her hands and began to sit on the floor.

'No, mother. Sit on the chair.'

Bebe took off her slippers and sat cross-legged in the chair.

'Memsahib, let me stay here until my son gets better.'

'No. It's not allowed by the hospital. You can see your son every day at four.'

'Yes, memsahib.'

Bebe slackened her jaw and turned back towards Karan.

Under the influence of medicine, Karan was still completely unconscious.

'Your son is sleeping right now. Just watch him, don't talk to him.' The nurse left.

Wide-eyed, Bebe looked at Karan, wrapped in white bandages, his body jaundiced and bruised.

'If anything happens to him, brother of Labho.'

In her mind, she was speaking to Lubhai's deceased father . . . as if Karan were the real son of Lubhai's mother and father.

'I will be broken.'

'Dayawanti.'

She had spoken to her neighbour before coming to the hospital. 'May you have a long life, Labho.'

'But that is wealth that doesn't belong to you. Your wealth is your own son.'

'Yes, sister. True wealth is the wealth that belongs to you. Karne has turned your world upside down.'

Bebe did the accounting in her head. Ever since Karne had got his job, he had given her three hundred rupees five times. At first, it was just gifts for show, but ever since he had gotten hundred-and-seventy-five-rupee bangles made for Lubhai, he was beside himself with joy.

'O Shivji, Bholenath! Save my Karne! I will make offerings of five and a quarter annas to the temple. O you who make things happen in the world, I will give my brass plate for your prayers. O lord of lords, every Monday I will listen to your tales. O . . .!'

The old woman sat for some time, praying for Karan. She pleaded for his life. Suddenly, she remembered that she had left the door to the house unlocked in her rush to come here. There were fifty-five rupees hidden in the earthenware pot. If someone found them then . . .

She got up from the chair. Lovingly, she caressed the bandages on Karan's forehead as he slept. She put on her slippers and left through the back door.

On the sixth day, he saw Dr Rana standing next to him.

'Hello, Mr Karan. Are you in any pain?'

'Oh . . . I . . . I . . .' Karan was addressing Dr Rana, but actually asking about Dr Bakhtiyar.

'Doctor Sahib came to see you on the first day.' Dr Rana explained to him. 'But on the second day, his own health took a turn for the worse.'

Karan was not feeling well today.

'Ha . . . O . . . I!' He was trying to ask Dr Rana, 'How is Doctor Sahib today?'

'Ever since that day, he has been unconscious. His mind is completely paralysed.'

After a while, Dr Rana spotted an old patient of his lying nearby and turned towards him.

'Dhani Ram, you've been admitted to the hospital?'

'Yes, doctorji. The doctor at the Social Service took pity on me and had me admitted. The money for the medicine . . .'

Dr Rana had already forgotten about Dhani Ram and had turned back to Karan.

'I don't know how long Dr Bakhtiyar can last in this condition. It would have been better if Zahra had not left so suddenly . . . I've sent a telegram to call Dr Bakhtiyar's brother here.'

'Oh . . . O . . . O!'

Karan wanted to shift a bit in bed, but he couldn't find the strength, so he just lay there . . .

'This brother of Doctor Sahib's seems to be a very generous man . . . Had Doctor Sahib remained conscious, he would have found a hundred ways to help you.'

It was as if Dr Rana were trying to justify not doing everything he could for Karan.

'Fazlu passed away. He was a very careless driver.' Dr Rana shrugged his shoulders and said, 'If . . . If I had been in the car, I would have . . .'

He imagined his wife wailing near the head of his corpse . . . Then his brother-in-law trying to comfort his wife. Then in a quavering voice, 'Okay, I will be going now.'

'Uncle Fazlu!' Karan said, as he felt his physical pain disappearing, making him forget his own existence.

'Karan Babu . . .'

Uncle Fazlu's spirit was sitting in front of Karan's bed on a windowsill, framed by light . . .

'If it can save someone's life, then by all means take all of my blood. Why didn't they take my blood . . .?'

'Karan Babu, I only have one regret. The doctor didn't take all of my blood.

'Karan Babu . . .!'

'Uncle . . .!'

Fazlu's spirit flew from the windowsill and came closer to Karan.

'If human blood is of no use to humans, then it is nothing! I only have one regret, Karan Babu. Had my blood not been spilt, it could have been of use to someone . . . It might have brought a mother back her child, and in her happiness she would uncontrollably . . . Ha ha ha ho . . . ho!'

And once again, Fazlu and Karan were sitting in the car, tumbling off the side of the Teetar Shah Bridge.

Once again, Karan let out a scream and then fell unconscious.

He was immediately taken to an operating theatre, where the surgeon, Habib, examined him, gave him an injection and conducted a quick inspection of his movements.

'Nurse, let him stay here. I think he will regain consciousness soon.'

'Doctor, his injuries are very serious. You have to get him blood one way or the other.'

'From where? His blood type is impossible to find.'

The surgeon, Habib, pensively lit a cigarette. He drew a chair to Karan's side and sat.

'After looking at his X-rays, I want to perform an operation on him today. There is a clear fracture visible in his skull that could cause his death any moment. But what can we do? It's very dangerous to perform even basic surgery on the skull without blood.'

'Have you tried the Social Service?'

'Social Service, Red Cross . . . We've asked all of them. But no one has his blood type.'

'Ask the People's Blood Bank, doctor.'

'Oh . . . O . . . O!'

When they heard Karan moaning, both turned to look at him.

'He will regain consciousness soon. But blood . . .?'

'People's Blood Bank . . .'

'I've asked them, too. Dr Shamsher Singh is aware that our patients are quite poor, and that's why he always puts us off.'

Karan opened his eyes, half-conscious, and stared at the two of them . . .!

'The People's Blood Bank has a lot of blood on reserve, doctor. Please try one more time. Try to save this innocent servant of God . . .!'

The surgeon shook his head sadly and stood up. He dialled the number for the People's Blood Bank from a phone in the corner of the room.

'Hello. Dr Shamsher Singh, please . . .?'

Karan imagined lying injured on a bed in the theatre of the People's Blood Bank and still selling his blood. His red blood was being squeezed out of him, flowing into glass tubes and pooling into the bottles belonging to the People's Blood Bank. The pallor of death spread across his face. He began to gasp for air as if his life was about to escape through his lips. His entire body grew stiff like a corpse's.

'Doctor! Doctor! Boy!'

Mrs Woolworth had sent Bacchu to call for Dr Shamsher Singh immediately.

'Doctor! Doctor!'

'Mrs Woolworth. What's the need for all of this commotion?'

Sardar Bahadur Dr Shamsher Singh entered the room.

'He . . . He's dying. Look, just examine his pulse!'

'Really?'

'If you like, we could give this man his own blood back. If he doesn't get his own blood back, he will die.'

'Give him back his own blood?'

The snake's tongue began flickering rapidly.

'That blood is something that I have purchased. It isn't stolen. And I mean to get its full price at one hundred and forty-five rupees per pint.'

'But . . . But . . .'

'No but-buts. One hundred and forty-five rupees per pint.'

Back in the operating room, the surgeon, Habib, put down the phone and turned to face Julia. 'Shamsher Singh says that finding that blood type is extremely difficult, but he can arrange for it at one hundred and forty-five rupees a pint.'

'Unfeeling brute! If all of the blood in the world were for sale like this then . . .'

Immediately, though, both turned their attention towards Karan at the same time . . .

The surgeon leapt to grab his wrist, trying to find his now-silent vein. He looked into lifeless eyes. Then, sadly shaking his head, he walked off to the side.

Through her tears, Julia stopped to look at the corpse. A depressing profile of life hanging its head defeatedly, completely still in its helplessness. Julia, then, prayed for the deceased. She made the sign of the cross across her chest and kissed her fingertips.

But she also started to think.

'This is not the time for kissing one's fingers. That's for old women who only know how to tremble in prayer. The time for kissing one's fingers is when you are trying to ward off the dark wings of the devil . . .'

Julia spread out the sheet with her helpless, quivering fingers. She covered Karan's motionless presence and turned towards the door.

Outside, Bebe, Hakeem Sukh Chen and Ragini had been standing, waiting. When they saw Julia's dejected face, they burst into tears.

Ragini's young child howled and cried, gesturing to his mother to take him into the operating theatre!

CHAPTER 14

After six days of being ill, Dr Manga came into his office at the Social Service League. When his assistant saw him, he said, 'Dr Habib called twice yesterday from Janta Hospital. They immediately need blood for a young man.'

'What blood type?'

'O negative. But we don't even have a single drop of blood of that type.'

'Oh, wait!' Dr Manga immediately remembered, 'Call Mr Karan at Dr Bakhtiyar's house. He has the same blood type.'

Satisfied, Dr Manga sat down in his chair. He thought about Karan for a little while and then said with a smile, 'What a good young man he is. He will come racing as soon as he hears that he is needed.'

Perhaps it was Karan's spirit hovering over him, dressed in the radiant robes of an angel.

MORE FROM PENGUIN

Angaaray

By Sajjad Zaheer, Ahmed Ali, Rashid Jahan and
Mahmud-Uz-Zafar

Translated by Snehal Shingavi

First published in 1932, this slim volume of short
stories created a firestorm of public outrage for its
bold attack on the hypocrisy of conservative Islam and
British colonialism. Inspired by British modernists like
Woolf and Joyce as well as the Indian independence
movement, the four young trailblazers who penned this
collection were eager to revolutionize Urdu literature.
Instead, they invited the wrath of the establishment:
the book was burned in protest and then banned by the
British authorities. Nevertheless, *Angaaray* spawned a
new generation of Urdu writers and gave birth to the
Progressive Writers' Association, whose members
included, among others, stalwarts like Chughtai,
Manto, Premchand and Faiz. This edition also provides
a compelling account of the furore surrounding this
explosive collection.

MORE FROM PENGUIN

Today's Pasts: A Memoir
By Bhisham Sahni
Translated by Snehal Shingavi

Rawalpindi in the first few decades of the twentieth century is a prosperous, bustling town, witnessing the first stirrings of the freedom movement. It is in this place and time that a delicate child grows into adolescence, at the heart of an unusual family. Adulthood and the horrific business of Partition drive the young man to Bombay, then Ambala and finally Delhi. As he gathers life experience and hones his talent at writing, his politics are formed. We observe the making of one of the icons of modern Hindi literature: Bhisham Sahni.

In addition to being the story of Sahni's life and art, *Today's Pasts* also chronicles the great cultural highpoints of modern India: the IPTA, the Progressive Writers' Association, the Nayi Kahani movement. The stars of Hindi and Urdu literature enter and exit the text as friends and familiars.

In Bhisham Sahni's hands a life story is transformed into a history of our present: one life bears witness to the tale of a nation.

MORE FROM PENGUIN

Shekhar: A Life

By Agyeya (S.H. Vatsyayan)

Translated by Snehal Shingavi and Vasudha Dalmia

On the night before he is to be hanged as a political prisoner, Shekhar finds himself drawn into a vortex of scattered memories—flashes of childhood angst and youthful love amidst days of high idealism and constant struggle against the British Raj. Enveloped by his past and wracked by a tumult of emotions, he muses on the philosophical questions that have consumed him and the ideological fervour that has led him to his inevitable fate. And as the appointed hour approaches, he must reconcile himself with who he has become and what he truly stands for.

Regarded as one of the most influential Hindi novels of all time, Shekhar powerfully reimagines the journey of an outspoken young underground revolutionary in pre-Independence India. This sparkling new translation brings to life the psychological acuity and literary richness of Agyeya's most profound work.